Camera 4

by
Martyn Ellington

This book is dedicated to
Reatha Ellington

My conscience, my inspiration, my
moral anchor

My Mam

Can you scan it?

It is said when the Wolfsbane blooms
and the moon is at its fullest,
even a man with the purest of hearts
can become the beast that dwells
within us all

1

Wales 1790

Evan Mawr ran hard and fast through the thick wet mud covering his farm yard, to the safety of his house. Every breath he took stung his lungs as they filled with the freezing night air of the Welsh hills, and every step became harder. His legs burned, the stitch in his side was agony, and he wanted to vomit. But the sight he'd just seen had filled him with terror, and he kept going. Evan knew if he stopped to rest, he would suffer the same fate as his livestock...

Earlier that day while Evan had been picking up supplies from the village, he'd heard about a stage coach which had been attacked by a large animal. 'As big as a horse,' Llywelyn Davies, the local inn-keeper, had told him. 'It tore into one of the horses and ripped it to shreds,' he had continued, but Evan had paid no mind to this tall tale. Llywelyn was known for exaggerating even the smallest of events. Evan thought that Llywelyn had found his true calling as an Inn Keeper, leaning over the bar and telling his tales to anyone who would listen. But it wasn't just Llywelyn who told this particular story. Robert Owain, the local police officer, or "Heddlu," as he preferred to be called, had been at the location of the supposed attack, but had seen nothing that would substantiate the story of a monster. There was a dead horse that had been pulled apart and eaten, but Robert had surmised that it had died of natural causes and the local wildlife had fed on it. Besides, Evan had grown up in these parts, taking the farm on when his father had died two winters ago. If there was anything supernatural going on he would know. Evan had said to Llywelyn, 'Don't you think at your age it's time to stop believing in monsters?' And with that he'd left the inn and travelled back up the mountainside to his farm.

The journey had taken some time, with only one horse. Evan was a hill farmer in the Denbigh area, and so he would never dare risk both of his horses pulling at the same time. If one became lame he always had the other tucked away safely inside the barn, so that he could swap them over if need be. His faithful sheep dog Elwy was with him, running ahead a little then stopping and turning back to look at him, as if to check that his master was still there. After a long cold hour sitting atop his cart, he pulled into his farm yard, unhitched Willow, his trusted Welsh pony, and lead her into her stable for the night. As he walked out, Perry, his only other horse, popped his head over his stable door. Evan stroked his nose and said,

'Don't worry lad, it's your turn next time. Best stay indoors tonight boy, the wind's getting up.'

He strolled towards his house, feeling the change in the weather. The temperature was starting to fall, with a wind chill being whipped up by a storm heading his way. Evan knew he should go and bring his sheep down from the grazing fields to lower slopes. But he also knew that first he had to have a hot drink and get warmed up before facing the task.

Elwy walked round his feet before laying next to him in front of the glowing fire. Evan looked down at his faithful dog and smiled at him. He'd had Elwy since he was a puppy, and over the 7 years they had worked together Elwy had become almost human to him. It seemed like the dog had a sense of what Evan wanted him to do. It had been a long time since Evan had needed to whistle commands to bring the sheep down or to heard them. Elwy was a master Shepard in his own right, and the bond and trust between them was unbreakable.

As Evan and Elwy left the house, Evan pulled the large oak door closed behind him. He didn't lock it; not here, and especially not at this time of the night. The only visitors he ever had were Robert on his patrols, or his long time friend Thomas Fychan. Evan always left the door open in case they called by, allowing them to go inside for a heat.

Interspersed across the dark night sky, the

lights of a million stars and the large full moon lit his way along the well trodden path that would lead them up to the higher grazing grounds. The air was clear and sharp. Evan could see the clouds of breath escaping Elwy's mouth as he ran ahead of him, again looking back just to be sure Evan was there. As they neared the crest of the hillside Evan noticed unusual tracks in the snow. They seemed large, almost dog-like in shape but bigger than any dog he had ever seen. As he placed his foot down next to one he realised they were longer than his own feet. He continued to step beside the tracks until he reached the crest of the hill and the gate that lead to the higher grazing field. Putting a hand on the gate latch, he continued to study the odd tracks. With a puzzled expression, he looked at Elwy.

'What's this then, lad?' he asked him, and as always Elwy seemed to answer him with a look of his own puzzlement.

As he unhitched the lock and started to swing the large gate open, he heard a sound he had not heard in the 7 years he'd had Elwy. His concentration shifted from the ground and he lifted his gaze up to where Elwy stood. The dog was still, rigid, his hackles standing erect on his back and shoulders, and his lips curled up; a deep menacing growl rumbling from the back of his throat. Evan hurried towards the dog and stayed at his side until they reached the clearing over the hill. There he saw a sight that made his blood run cold. There was nothing but carnage before him. His heard of sheep lay in frozen pools of their own blood; carcases ripped from head to tail, dismembered limbs and heads strewn across the field. He just stood there, not knowing what to do.

Evan had seen the odd sheep taken by large dogs before, mostly walkers with dogs they couldn't control. It was expected that he would lose two or three a season, but even on such occasions the dogs had gone for the throat and then left the sheep intact. No, this was something different. His whole flock had been massacred. Butchered. Suddenly he noticed something move in the far corner of his eye. He couldn't make out exactly what it was, he only saw the outline. He noticed large plumes of breath escaping from the figure's mouth, and as the moonlight shone down from behind it he could make out tangled, matted grey hair. Then Evan saw its size. The shock made him gasp. Whatever this figure was, it was massive. Bigger than any animal he'd seen before. He strained his eyes to see better, and noted that its stance had changed. No longer did it seem to be standing side on, looking at him from the other side of the field. Now it seemed to be standing straight, its head bowed down. He could see its huge shoulders moving, then he realised with horror that it was walking towards him. Evan started to move backwards, ushering Elwy with his hand, to do the same.

'C'mon boy, lets go,' he said to the dog, as calmly as he could.

But Elwy did not move.

'Elwy, lets go. C'mon now!'

But the dog stood his ground. He looked back up across the field to see the shape growing in size.

Evan knew he had to turn and run. He just had to hope that Elwy would do the same. He fled back down the hillside, guided only by the stars and the moon and his memory of this track; a track he had walked all his life. He dared a fleeting glance back but Elwy was nowhere to be seen.

'Elwy!' he yelled, but he couldn't hear the sound of the dog's paws patter on the protruding rocks, or the crisp crushing of the snow as he brushed through it. As the ground started to level out and he could see the distant lights of his farm house, he pushed on and shouted again, 'Elwy!' Then he heard the sound he dreaded: The unmistakable sound of a dog growling and fighting, quickly followed by a yelp of pain, and then nothing. But while Evan felt great sadness for his dog, he also knew that nothing now stood between him and the animal that had slaughtered his sheep...

At last he reached his door. His last steps across

the thick, sticky mud had left him weak and worn out. He reached for the door handle, knowing he had no time to fiddle with it. This had to be an all-in-one attempt to turn the handle and push the door open. He knew the creature was behind him. Whatever this animal - this monster - was, it had gained ground on him with ease and now he feared it was toying with him. If he didn't get in right away, it would surely snatch him back into the darkness and tear him to pieces as it had done with his sheep. His hand smacked against the handle and in one swift movement he turned it and pushed the heavy solid door open. He burst through, into his house, spinning around as quickly as he could, fighting for every last piece of breath and strength as he slammed the door shut and put his full weight behind it.

The impact he was expecting came seconds after. Evan was a big man - a farmer all his life. He was a strong powerful man, but the impact had driven him back as the door was forced open. He pushed back against it and managed to get the top dead bolt in place just as the second impact came. The frame rattled, and years of dust that had collected between it and the thick walls, exploded out. Evan dropped down, pushing in the bottom bolt and securing the lock. That was it now, he could do no more than pray and hope that the door would keep the thing out.

BANG! It hit the door again and again. The frame rattled. More dust fell from the gaps. Evan walked backwards into his kitchen, searching for anything he could arm himself with. He reached out a hand and grasped the poker he used to keep his fire going, still watching the door intently. As another hit came he reached his dining table. BANG! Another blow. The door creaked and groaned under the force. He crouched under the table, clasping the poker, turning his knuckles white. Sweat ran down his back, and he shook with fear, praying for his life as he curled up and waited for the door to yield.

One more bang hit the door, but it held. The top bolt now started to bend; the screws that held the strike to the frame were starting to pull out under the massive force. For a few moments all fell silent. Evan was still cowering under the table, not daring to believe it was finally over. He exhaled, letting go of the breath he'd held in for so long, and he relaxed his grip on the poker, allowing blood to return to his knuckles. Breathing as quietly as he could he stared at the door, still shaking, adrenaline still rushing around inside him. Then a frightening thought filled his mind, and his body tensed again. Would it find another way in? Panic coursed around his body, and the shallow breathing and tight grip on the poker returned. He tried to convince himself it couldn't come in the windows, as they were far too small for such a large animal to fit through. 'No,' he told himself. 'The only way in is through that door.' The silence continued, and once again Evan allowed himself to relax. He moved his gaze from the door; he had to check the windows even though he believed with absolute conviction, that they were too small. But he had to look. What small amount of strength and reserve he had, he used to turn his head and look out from his hiding place.

There it stood, this creature; this monster that he had told Llywelyn only a few hours ago, didn't exist. It was staring right at him. He could see it was standing on its hind legs. Its front legs, which it now used for arms, were reaching over the top of the window frame, allowing its massive head to bend down and glare in at him. As it stood snorting and sniffing the air around the window, its breath condensed against the cold glass, adding to the fear that now tightly gripped Evan. Rough tangled grey hair covered its long snout, and its curling, thick black lips revealed its forward teeth glistening in the bright moonlight. Massive fangs hung down, saliva dripping from them, and its eyes were set deep into its skull. Framed against the dark grey fur that surrounded them, Evan saw that the eyes were full of hatred, evil; death. But what filled him with fear above everything else, was the colour of this godless creature's eyes. They weren't the brown eyes of a normal animal or the red eyes that demons were believed to have. These eyes were blue, and they looked human. The creature seemed to stare at him for an eternity, and he felt its gaze reach down into his soul. It seemed as if terrorizing him physically wasn't enough for this thing; it also wanted to haunt him and invade his mind, perhaps even his dreams. Evan closed his eyes tightly.

'Please God make it go, make it go!'

He dared to open his eyes.

The window was clear. He sighed as he curled up under the table once more, but the silence and peace he'd hoped for, didn't last. The air soon filled with cries and screams of pain. The screams came from his barn but there was nothing he could do.

Evan woke to a bang on the door. Crying out in fear, he snatched hold of the poker and readied himself again, but as he became more awake and aware, he realised with relief that it was morning. Light was streaming in from the window that last night had framed the face of horror. Bang, bang again.

'Evan, are you in lad?'

It was Robert.

'Evan, come on now, open up.'

Evan now recognised the voice of his friend Thomas. He climbed out from his hiding place and walked to the door. As he swung the door open the bottom edge scraped against the floor. He looked up to see the bent and twisted hinges that had no doubt saved his life last night.

'What happened here?' Robert asked him.

Evan walked past his friends without saying a word, and looked towards the barn. Its doors had been ripped off and thrown across the farm yard. He started to make his way towards it, but Thomas placed a hand on his shoulder.

'Don't go in there Evan, that's not something you should see.'

He turned to face Thomas, and smiled his thanks for his concern, then he stepped away from him and entered the barn. He stopped dead at the entrance, and brought his hand up to his mouth, biting down on his fist. The smell was unbearable. His horses had met with the same fate as his sheep. His pigs lay scattered around the barn; entrails still stuck to the side of the building and hung from posts close to where they had been ripped out of the animals and flung aside.

Thomas walked in behind him. 'Evan,' he said softly to him, 'what happened here? What did this?'

Evan shook his head and wiped the tears from his eyes. 'A beast,' was the only reply that came, and it came in a mournful whisper. 'There's more. Follow me.'

Evan started up the hill that would lead him,

Thomas and Robert to the field where the sheep had been killed. Nothing was said between them as they made their way up the path. Eventually they reached the gate that led into the field. It was still open, exactly as Evan had left it last night when he had run for his life. He stepped though it and came upon the body of Elwy. He sank to his knees and cradled him. Elwy wasn't like the others; the body was still intact but the odd angle of the dog's head told him that his neck had been broken. Thomas knelt beside him. Looking across the field, a feeling of shock and total disbelief now washed over him. He turned back to Evan.

'What did this? What happened to Elwy?'

Evan stood up, holding his dog's body, and began to carry it back down the hillside. 'It was a beast, Thomas. Straight from hell. A monster. The one that attacked the coach. It came for us both, but Elwy...' He gestured down at the dead dog he carried in his arms. 'He protected me to the end. It would have got me too, but Elwy saved my life. He fought it. He gave me enough time to get away.'

Robert followed behind them, listening to Evan's story as he explained the events of the previous night.

As they reached the farm house Evan lay the dead dog on the ground and turned to his two friends. 'If you'll excuse me, I want to bury Elwy.'

'And then what?' Thomas asked. 'You'll need help rebuilding your farm.'

Evan stared at him and frowned. 'Rebuild? No, Thomas, I'm not staying here, not now. The beast knows I'm here. It'll come back for me, you see.'

Thomas's voice started to rise, not with anger but with concern for his friend. 'But what will you do? Where will you go?'

'To Cardiff. To the city. I'll be safer there. There's safety in numbers.'

'When?'

'Today, as soon as I'm done here. Now leave me to do this. I must be gone before the night returns, and that... that devil comes back for me.'

He turned his back on them both and waved them away. Thomas wanted to stay. He wanted to talk his friend out of leaving, but Robert put a heavy hand on his shoulder and pulled him away.

'Come on lad,' he said quietly. 'Best leave him be. We'll come back tomorrow. He'll still be here, he's just upset.'

With that, Thomas and Robert left Evan and headed back towards the village.

Under the winter's sun Evan buried Elwy below the large tree they'd sat beneath in the hot summer days, now forever behind them. He said a few words, and wiped more tears from his face. Back at the house he packed what he could carry and left. He stopped in the doorway and took one last look into the house. The heavy iron poker still lay on the floor, under the table, and the image of the face at the window shot back into his mind. He pulled shut the door that had kept him alive. He locked it, turned and left the farm behind. After that day no-one ever saw or heard of Evan again. No trace of him was ever found. He simply ceased to exist.

2

Portland USA, present day

Myth Seekers was a long running TV show created by its producer and presenter Connar Taylor. He had started the show on Public Access TV, and over the years he'd built its following until only a year ago a major network had picked up the programme, following the success of other similar shows. The format was easy: the team - mainly made up by people Connar knew - looked for myths and legends and then travelled to that particular part of the world with a host of high-tech instruments, to see if they could be proved. As with all these types of TV shows, Connar's *Myth Seekers* had never found concrete evidence of anything they had investigated.

In the early days they investigated only local folklore and legends, such as the Witches Castle - the sight of the first hanging in Portland - simply because none of them could afford the instruments needed or the travel costs to fly around the world. But now they had a large network picking up the tab, it seemed that nowhere was off limits. Their most recent case, from which they'd just returned, involved looking for giant worms in the Gobi desert. The locals claimed that the mutant worms ate their animals, and sometimes even their relatives! The trip had been exhausting, as were most of these trips to destinations that had little or no infrastructure to speak of, and even less of the home comforts the team were used to. But Connar and his crew enjoyed their work and often commented on how they had "the best job in the world."

As they arrived back at their base they followed the usual protocol of unpacking the equipment to check it and clean it, and then dispatching what little traces of evidence they had found to specialists and pathology labs for a professional opinion. Once this had been returned, Connar and his team would then go back into the studio to record the findings from the previous show, and set up the next show by presenting the legend or myth they would be investigating. Finding the myths to investigate fell to Ruby Lauren, a long time friend of Connar. They had met in college, and Ruby was one of the original members on the Public Access show. Her main responsibility was finding interesting and original myths or legends and bringing them to the attention of the team. From there they would decide which one sounded more likely to produce good TV, and then present it on the air. Connar trusted Ruby's attention to detail and her investigation work. Not once had she sent them to a place where none of the locals had heard of the thing they'd come to find. She always managed to seek out obscure myths and legends that were generally unheard of, and incredible stories often passed down through generations. Ruby knew what the viewers wanted, and Connar was very grateful for her intuitive good judgement. He wasn't so grateful for her fiery temper however. At only 5'2", with long red hair, Connar was sure she would be a match for any monster or ghost they might come across. But Ruby's temperament was beneficial to Connar; it meant he didn't have to worry about the rest of the team pulling their weight. He didn't have to involve himself in the little misunderstandings and tantrums that inevitably occurred. He could quite easily leave these things to Ruby while he concentrated on running the show and keeping the Network executives (or "Puppets," as he called them) happy.

They had been back in Portland for two weeks now, and all the evidence of the giant worm had been collected. As usual nothing conclusive was present, apart from some strange markings in the sand, which couldn't be accounted for even with the casts they had made, and some noises they had recorded during the night. Their contact at the Oregon Zoo couldn't match the sounds to anything specific, but did comment on the fact that "they could just be locals messing around with you." Connar had called the team to the *Myth Seekers* studio set, and as always Ruby had some new cases to look at. They would decide on air, which to follow up. Of course they had already had the meeting back stage with the six cases Ruby had brought in, and they had already decided on the two they would discuss on air and the one they would actually follow up on, but discussing them on air made good TV. It seemed to make the show more authentic, and most importantly it filled up some time. The less they had to talk about regarding the last case, the more they could discuss the new one. The format hadn't changed at all since its early days. Connar would introduce the programme, and then his team, after which the discussions would take place and the video tape - or VT as the insiders called it – would be shown. As the timer counted down to the air time, (even though the show was recorded and played out later that week it still had to be counted in), the crew took their places and the floor manager counted them in:

'And in 5,4,3.' For the counts 2 and 1 the floor manger used only her hands to make sure her voice was not picked up.

As Connar watched her count down to 1 the red light came on and the show began.

'Welcome to *Myth Seekers*, with me Connar Taylor, and my crew of investigators.'

The camera panned round as each crew

member waved, then went back to Connar.

'Over the last few years we've tracked some strange and wonderful places looking for some strange and wonderful creatures, and last week's episode was no different. We went looking for the giant man-eating worm that's said to roam the Gobi Desert.'

'And cut,' shouted the floor manager. 'Okay Connar that's fine, we'll cut the VT in there and we'll film the rest of the show in 10 minutes.'

Connar nodded and turned to Howard Green, his field technical director. 'Did the new FLIR camera come in yet?'

'Yeah,' Howard said, nodding as he smiled. This new camera was the crowning jewel in Howard's growing collection of expensive and highly technical equipment. The FLIR camera - or *Forward Looking Infra-red Radiometer* - allowed Howard to see in the dark by illuminating any heat sources in red, making them stand out against the dark blue and green background of the cold surroundings. 'I've checked it out already, it's awesome. It's like having cats' eyes.'

'Cool,' Connar said. 'I'm glad you're getting the best equipment these days.' He valued Howard's technical ability. It was often Howard who ultimately provided what little evidence they managed to gather.

The floor manager called them back to their spots to continue taping the show, and began the countdown again.

'And in 5,4,3.' Then the hand signals 2 and 1, then the red lights, and Connar started the next part of the show - the part that would follow on the VT of their last trip.

'And so, as you can see, we did hear noises that can't be explained, and we took casts of some prints in the sand that we can't match to anything. Although we didn't see the man-eating worm, who knows what's really out there under the sands in the Gobi Desert? Okay, moving on to something a little closer to home. In Europe - to the United Kingdom, and more specifically, Wales. Ruby, what do you have for us?'

The camera switched to Ruby and she took over the presenting.

'Well Connar, I think I may have a particularly interesting myth here. The locals around the town of Denbigh in Wales, claim that a large wolf-like animal has stalked those parts for over 300 years. There have been recent sightings, and an increase in certain strange phenomena in the area.'

The camera switched back to Connar.

'Sounds intriguing, Ruby.'

He turned and looked at Melanie Ward. Mel was the field sound engineer, but like Ruby, she helped out with presenting the show and always introduced the other story.

'Yes Connar, Ruby's wolf legend sounds fascinating, but I have a ghost story here that may well keep you awake at night. It's said that Poveglia - a small Island in Venice, Italy - is one of the most haunted spots in the world. It's documented that during the outbreak of the Bubonic Plague in 1576, all of Venice's dead were taken to the Island and the bodies left there to rot. It's off limits and patrolled by police, but those who've secretly made the crossing have often been scared off the island by ghostly sightings and terrifying sounds. And the strangest thing of all, which can't be explained, is that nothing will grow around there, and birds never fly over the area.'

The camera panned back to Connar.

'Fascinating, Mel. What do the rest of us think? It's between a large wolf-like creature and ghosts of the plague victims.'

The camera panned out to encompass the whole team, who then went into a pre-planned and pre-scripted improvisation style of conversation about the merits of each case, until they decided that the case in Wales was the preferred one. With that, the camera closed in tightly on Connar.

'Okay, it looks like we're going to the UK to look for Ruby's wolf legend. This is the last show in the current series. Be sure to join us next series when we'll be back on air with our results. Meantime, we're off on the hunt for a giant wolf in Wales. Goodbye and thanks for watching.'

'And cut,' shouted the floor manager.

In the background the show's music played and the credits rolled up the monitors surrounding the small studio set.

Connar called the group together.

'Okay everyone, ready to go?'

They all nodded and smiled eagerly.

'Mel, what are the travel arrangements?'

Mel had made the arrangements before they recorded the show.

'Okay, we fly from Portland International to JFK New York, with Jetblue Airways, and then we have a stop-over before our Virgin Atlantic flight to London, England, at 6.30 tomorrow evening. We pick up our vehicle at the airport, then drive to Denbigh in Wales. I'm told it's about a five hour drive.'

Connar smiled his appreciation, and lightly placed his hand on her back as the group gathered round. 'Okay guys,' he said, 'I'll see you all at the airport tomorrow at 5 o'clock. Make sure you've got everything you need.'

Philip Hughes, the team's cameraman, was the first to arrive at the airport terminal. Phil was another long time friend of Connar's. Standing 6'4 he was by far the tallest of the group, and by far the thinnest. His long, almost skeletal frame had been the cause of much bullying in school, and the fact that he was the resident film geek didn't help his cause now. But that didn't matter to Phil, and it hadn't mattered back then, though the insults were much easier to deflect than the many over-enthusiastic blows the "Jocks" had landed him during gym. Phil was a loner. Maybe that was why Connar had taken him under his wing and befriended him. They had much in common. In Phil, Connar could see some of his own insecurities. Secretly he was as much of a film buff as Phil, and they'd often had heated exchanges about the best fight scene or death scene in various movies. But they agreed on which were the best movies ever made. When Connar had had the idea for the show, Phil was the one cameraman he'd wanted on board. And Phil hadn't needed much persuading.

Dressed in his trademark jeans and long sweatshirt, he hauled his camera equipment through the airport. It was equipment that not so long ago he had only dreamed of operating. But now, with the network's money and resources, Phil used the latest Sony PMW-EX3 camera with all the latest features, including remote control and removable flash memory. Now he could take the sort of shots he had always wanted to. But even with his new "toy," Connar still held him back from making his work too professional and clean. In Connar's view the show had to retain its original raw feeling that the viewers liked so much. Even so, Phil still loved his new kit and kept it clean in an almost obsessional way.

He stood waiting in the large viewing area, watching the planes outside take off and land. Hundreds - even thousands - of people, climbing into aluminium tubes and trusting their lives to someone they had never met and would never meet. The information boards continued to flash back and forth, announcing each flight due in or out and its present position. 'This call is for passengers of flight 939 Portland to Atlanta to begin boarding.' As the voice announced the boarding of another flight, Phil watched an average looking man in an off the peg suit walk to his gate. He smiled and relaxed back against the wall, thankful he was not in such a rush. The large bags containing his equipment sat securely on the airport trolley. With one hand resting on them, there was no way in hell anybody would get to his precious camera.

Howard arrived next, with the usual assortment of bags and holdalls. Phil watched him as he approached. Before the show Howard and Phil hadn't known each other. It was Connar who'd brought them together. Howard had met Connar through a mutual friend, and after discussing their shared interest in all things mysterious and mythological, they had decided to start the show. The set up was easy; Howard - who came from a wealthy family - provided the money and Connar, the talent. The rest of the team consisted of

Connar's friends and acquaintances with similar interests.

Howard wasn't a tall man, nor was he particularly broad. He was, in most respects, exactly how one would imagine a privately educated man from a rich family, to look. From his perfectly cut dark-blond hair down to his expensive designer shoes, he oozed elegance, charm and effortless style. As he walked towards Phil, he smiled.

'Hi Phil, how are you today?'

'I'm good. Seems we got here before the others.'

'Yeah, looks like it,' Howard said, as he looked around for any other members of their party. He stood next to Phil, pulling his own trolley alongside his colleague's. 'You all set to go?'

Phil gently patted his collection of bags. 'Sure am. Got my new camera and harness in here. I'm not letting it out of my sight! How about you?'

Howard reached forward and picked up a case from the top of his pile of bags. 'Got my FLIR camera, remote cameras and heat seekers, we got laptops, we got satellite feeds and we got infra-red lenses. I think between us if there is an over-sized wolf up there, we'll definitely find it!'

Howard put the bag back down and smiled reassuringly at Phil. Both men were very proud of their high-tech equipment. They had every right to be - the network had spared no expense in giving Connar and his crew what they had asked for. *Myth Seekers* was one of their top-rated shows, and they knew that the better the technical side; the better the results. Good results made good TV.

Connar arrived next, with Melanie and Ruby. As usual Ruby looked like someone with purpose and direction; her no-nonsense single nod of acknowledgement to Howard and Phil was the minimum required to say a, 'Hi guys, how are you doing?' But neither of them responded in kind. Ruby was met with a giddy and somewhat over-enthusiastic 'Hi Ruby,' but in her way she appreciated it and smiled coyly, before focusing on handing out the boarding passes and tickets for the flights.

After checking in their equipment, they passed their time in the usual shops and coffee houses that were typically present in every airport. The team sat together in one such coffee shop, talking over the plans for the show and the format for the up-and-coming investigation. The show they had recorded the previous day wouldn't be aired until the following week, by which time they would be high on the Welsh hills. They had to be guarded in their discussions: they were now recognised by the public - a fact they didn't take lightly - and any overheard conversations about the project in Wales would soon be sweeping around the web, making the whole investigation and subsequent show somewhat pointless. Connar sat forward in his large leather armchair - one of several miss-matched chairs which had been carefully chosen by the branding department, to make the surroundings look casual yet stylish - and which were placed neatly around a low, solid oak table. He put his large Mocha down, whilst gently leaning towards Ruby.

'So, how authentic is this wolf legend we're chasing?'

Ruby smiled knowingly, and ushered the others to huddle around the table. 'Very, actually. The farmer who made the report to the local police, and his friend - who, by the way, found him cowering under the kitchen table - were adamant that a large grey monster with blue human-like eyes, had slaughtered his livestock and killed his dog. But it happened a while back – in 1790.'

Howard caught Ruby's attention. 'Given that this happened over 200 years ago, is it still worth looking in to? Have there been any other sightings since then? I mean, even if there was some kinda rogue wolf running around, it would have been dead long ago, wouldn't it?'

'You'd think so,' Ruby said, 'but what makes this case the one to follow is this: After the farmer had fled, reports died off, then suddenly started again after 20 years. The wolf - or whatever - seemed to head towards the border with England. Towards....oh, what do you call it?' Ruby tapped her head with her index finger - a sure sign she was concentrating and didn't want to be interrupted. Suddenly she sprang back in full flow. 'Cheshire, that's it. Then the whole thing died out again for over a hundred years, until mutilated sheep and cattle started to show up in the 1920's, the 50's and again the 90's, back in Wales, near the Denbigh area.'

Howard said, 'But even the 90's is twenty years ago, Ruby.'

Ruby's expression changed to frustration as she cut across him. 'Yes Howard, but four weeks ago a tourist walking in the hills, found a fully-grown dairy cow ripped from front to back, and so far the Welsh authorities haven't come up with any explanation. Hence the legend has come back to life and the locals are now afraid that the beast has returned.'

Ruby sat back in her own oddly matched leather chair, and smiled contentedly.

Howard looked at Phil. 'What do you think?'

Phil forced a nervous smile. 'I guess we're moving up in the world.'

'What do you mean?' Melanie asked.

He turned to face her across the table. 'Well, normally we chase down ghost stories or giant worms that are supposed to create havoc in small towns, with no hope of ever finding them.'

'So why's this different?' Mel asked.

'Because this isn't some back-water town in the deep south, or tribesmen in the middle of the Gobi desert. This is a large town in a developed country that borders England. This legend may actually have some real substance. Oh, I don't mean some huge wolf running around, but I've heard of big cats living wild over there. You never know guys, we may find our legend this time.'

Mel sighed, and leaned back in her chair to think it over.

'But none of the reports..."

Ruby was interrupted by the PA system calling them to their gate and the first part of their long journey.

Connar led them through the gate and onto the aircraft. Ruby - as efficient as always - had placed Howard, Phil and Mel across the centre seats while she and Connar took the window seats, allowing them to discuss in finer detail the layout and format for this particular investigation without any disturbance from others. The plane taxied, and with a roar from its twin jet engines it hurtled down the runway until the rumbling of the tyres ended and they felt the pressure of the take-off pushing them back into their seats. After climbing and turning onto the flight path, the engines quietened and a low, soothing calm came about the passenger compartment.

'Hey Ruby, can you show me the research

you've done?' Connar asked

Ruby pulled out her folder, titled,"Welsh Werewolf," and handed it to him.

Connar was surprised by the title of the file. *'Welsh Werewolf?* I thought it was just a large wolf?'

'Probably is,' she said, 'but I thought it sounded more dramatic. Besides, you're not scared of some crazy Werewolf legend, are you?'

Connar smiled and shook his head. 'No, of course not. Werewolves aren't real. But it might make a good title for the episode.'

'Yeah, that's what I thought. There's nothing like Werewolf or Vampire in the title to get people watching.'

She turned her attention to the small laptop screen in front of her, and left him to browse her notes.

Connar opened the file and started to go through it. While Ruby ran a tight ship and was always dependable, he didn't like the idea that she knew more than he did about the facts of any legend they investigated. Not because he felt insecure about it, but because as the team leader - and he guessed the boss of the outfit - he always felt he should know as much if not more than anyone else.

The flight continued without incident, eventually touching down in JFK where they boarded the 747 which would take them on to

London. Once the plane had reached its cruising speed and height, and was flying almost without sensation other than the low hum of the four huge Rolls Royce jet engines, Connar settled back into his seat. Looking round the dimmed cabin, he noted that most of the passengers were falling asleep. Those still awake were either reading or watching a movie on the small LED screens in front of them. He turned to Ruby, but she had already pulled down her eye shield and cuddled into her complimentary pillow and blanket. Still too awake to sleep but too sleepy to watch any of the movies available, he pulled the research file back out of his hand luggage and started reading it again.

3

The file read:

Anyone who watches the late night horror channel knows that werewolves are human by day and turn into a rabid monster hungry for human blood when the moon is full, and that only a silver bullet can kill them. This of course is fiction made up by Hollywood in the early years of movies to make the audience feel that should they ever be faced with such a creature there was at least some way of killing it.

Of course the real legend of the werewolf differs somewhat from the sliver screen, it is said that once a human is turned and goes through the changes they can never take the human form again, for once the beast is released it can never be brought back under control, and as for the silver bullet, well legends tell that the only real way to kill a werewolf is to severe the head from body and only then will it turn back to the person it once was, which could explain why a dead werewolf has never been found but decapitated people have.

There are many legends of such creatures around the world. From South America where it's called the Chupacabra, which is a small but fierce creature through to the full blown huge werewolves of Transylvania. Little however has been documented about such a beast that is said to wonder the hills and moors around the Denbigh area of Wales. For over 200 years locals and travellers alike have reported strange sounds in the night and mutilated cattle and livestock, there have even been cases of missing hill walkers and tourists over the years. It started in 1791 when a hill farmer went into his higher fields to bring his sheep down for the night and found them mutilated, it is said that when his friend found him the next day he was cowering under his kitchen table holding a fire poker tight in his hand and that he kept saying he'd seen the devil and that it would come back for him. Even his faithful dog had been killed by this supernatural creature which is thought to have chased down the hillside after him. But because he managed to lock himself in his farm house the beast then exacted its fury on the farm yard animals which were torn apart and flung around the barn. The next day we're told he buried his dog and disappeared never to be heard from again, and his farm was left to fall into ruin.

Locals of the area also tell of a stage coach that was attacked and one of its horses been torn limb from limb. The attack is said to haven take place after sunset when there was a blood red, the locals back then called it a blood moon which they took as a sign of evil. We now know it was due to dust in the upper atmosphere from a forest fire.

It was seven years later before the next sighting was reported; two men hill walking saw something tracking them that made them run for their lives. They found shelter in an inn and refused to leave until the morning. Later that day the mutilated bodies of two homeless men were found just 5 miles from the inn. An anonymous letter was left for the local minister claiming the men had been killed by a werewolf and that it was the same one that had attacked the stage coach and the farmer.

The attacks gradually died out until two centuries later when new attacks by a large unknown animal were reported again. A Welsh newspaper reported sightings of a strange bear like creature that had been seen by a farmer during a full moon after which he had found two of his healthy 70 pound lambs ripped apart.

Further sightings in 1992 and 1994 caught the attention of London zoo who gave the locals two steel cages that were used for capturing and holding Polar Bears. The cages were bated with meat and left over the moons cycle. When they were checked two days later one of the traps had been activated and the meat was gone. Unfortunately what ever it had trapped had ripped the cage open from the inside and escaped. The zoo was at a loss to explain how this could have happened as they were designed to hold Polar Bears the largest and strongest land carnivore. However there were tracks left by whatever creature it was and casts were taken. The casts were sent to an American expert who claims the prints strongly resembled the fossilised prints left by the long extinct Sabre-Tooth Tiger which has not roamed Britain for over two million years. He went to say nothing that he knows of that walks the earth today could leave such tracks and rip apart a bear cage from the inside.

Of course all these stories and testimonies make for

good bedtime reading, but if you're ever in the Denbigh area during a full moon and you hear strange noises or you come across mutilated animals it may be a good idea to head for an inn.

Connar lowered the file papers to his lap, and sighed. He had been on his fair share of cases by now, going back to the early days on a public network. They had investigated nearly 150 legends, but he had always known even before they'd gotten to the destination, that the legend was a story that had simply gotten out of control over the years, passed down by generations and exaggerated along the way to ensure it still shocked. As each generation had passed, it had become harder and harder to scare a people, so the legends had had to become more and more horrific. But this case seemed different somehow. It was hardly known, compared with The Loch Ness Monster or even the Gobi Desert worms they had just investigated. There was far more proof and evidence that this thing could actually exist in some form.

As he stared out of the plane's small oval window at the now pitch black view, he assured himself that, while there were some who thought that large cats *did* roam parts of Britain, perhaps illegally owned then released by their owners who couldn't cope when their small cute pets had grown, he also knew that such wild cats tried to keep away from people.

In modern times there had been more people killed by cows in Britain, than by wild big cats. Connar concluded that the forthcoming expedition would be just like the rest - good TV, good entertainment, but completely safe and unfounded. After all, there was no such thing as a werewolf. With that final thought, he convinced himself not to take Ruby's notes too literally. He settled down on the pillow, pulled the blanket over himself and fell into a deep, restful sleep.

The flight touched down at Heathrow, London, the following morning. Connar and his crew got through custom control with their bags and equipment, without any problems, then headed for the car rental company to collect the keys for the minibus. The pretty young woman behind the desk smiled the usual "customer service" smile as she completed the paperwork, checked their insurance and licences, and proceeded in her best non-condescending tone to remind them to drive on the left side of the road.

'Your car is parked in bay E11. Have a safe journey. Next please...'

Connar slid the keys from her open hand and smiled back at her, trying to put some kind of human element into the proceedings. This was a typical start to a trip: Every country had the same clerk behind the same desk saying the same shit. A robot with a plastic smile, repeating their own particular set of rules and regulations.

When they reached bay E11 they found the silver Ford Galaxy parked neatly, waiting for them. As the others loaded their equipment and climbed into the car, Connar took the driver's seat and fired up the diesel engine. Engaging first gear with the stick shift, he set off when everyone was ready, and followed the instructions from the on-board Satellite Navigation system. The journey around London's M25 circular road was as eventful and irritating as it was for the millions of people who used it to commute every day of the week - a journey plagued by road works, traffic jams, speed cameras and police patrol cars travelling just under the speed limit, with most drivers hesitant to overtake them.

They eventually left London behind and headed towards the border with Wales. After 5 hours of travelling, interrupted by a few stops, they headed into Llanrhaeadr - a small village between Denbigh and Wrexham, and the place where the legend had begun over 200 years before. Connar pulled the Galaxy into the hotel car park. Their hotel was an old inn aptly named The Old Inn - a white-washed stone building set back from the only main road that travelled through the small village. As they unloaded the car they were overawed by the absolute beauty and Britishness of the village.

Across the road was the village church, complete with cemetery. A little farther down the road was a traditional red phone booth. Standing proudly beside the phone box was a quintessential, bright red British mail box. This village was exactly how most foreign visitors would imagine a small British village to be, and it was probably how they'd expect all towns to look, given the image and stereotyping that Hollywood portrayed of life in Britain.

'This is great,' Connar remarked as he headed towards the inn door.

'Glad you approve,' Ruby replied, smiling at the rest of the group who now followed Connar through the small door and into the cramped, dimly lit bar. Flag stones provided a floor - no doubt put down when the inn was originally built as a coach house, centuries ago. The stones were now smooth and uneven after many years and many feet passing over them. Towards the bar, dark-wood beams stretched across the low ceiling, and a collection of dust-covered plates and various stuffed animals littered the high shelves all around the roughly plastered walls. At the end of the bar an open fire crackled and snapped as it burned. Ash lay scattered around the hearth. Close to the fire were three large wing-back chairs arranged around a small, round, three legged wooden table. Connar approached the bar, offering his hand for a welcome shake. He then leaned in to speak to the bar tender.

'Hi, I'm Connar Taylor. We have three rooms booked for tonight.'

The barman shook his hand firmly. He'd recognised the television star immediately. 'Pleased to meet you. Three rooms, you say? Hang on, I'll check with the wife. She does the booking, you see.'

He disappeared through the small arch that led from the bar. Connar looked back at his crew and smiled, shrugging his shoulders. He noticed two older men sitting in a dark corner, just left of the fireplace. They stared back at him before looking at each other then taking another sip of their ale. They must be locals, Connar surmised. People from the village, no doubt, related to the families who'd lived and worked these areas for generations.

His attention was snapped back by the bar tender's return.

'Here's your keys, Mr. Taylor," he said as he held out his hand, this time with three brass keys in his palm. 'The rooms are just up the stairs.' He pointed past the two locals, to a small but heavy-looking door.

'It's Connar. Do you need my credit card?'

'Credit card?' The barman laughed. 'We don't take those things here lad, just pay tomorrow when you leave.'

Connar smiled politely, and took the keys. He handed Ruby and Howard a key each.

'So, who's with who?' asked Mel.

Connar gestured towards Ruby. 'You're with Ruby, Phil's with Howard and I have a room to myself.'

'Typical,' Phil protested with a hint of sarcasm and a crooked smile.

Connar replied as he headed for the small heavy-looking door. 'I'm the boss, I get the room.'

The team made their way to their rooms and made themselves as comfortable as possible in the rather basic accommodation. It was agreed that they would meet back in the bar at 7pm. that evening. With the time difference and the long drive after their flights they all felt drained, and what they wanted more than anything before their planned two nights in the field, was a hot bath and hot meal, followed by a good night's sleep.

Connar checked his watch. He had time for a quick nap before meeting the others for dinner. He pulled the velvet curtains across his first floor window, undressed and climbed into the large wooden-framed bed that sat proudly in the middle of his room. He pulled the sheet up over his shoulders and snuggled under heavy blankets, and fell asleep immediately.

Connar found himself walking out of his bedroom door, but as he did he was outside and on the moors. Clouds moved silently across a darkened sky with only the light of the large full moon, Mel and

Howard stood next to him pointing ahead. He looked in the direction and saw a beast stood atop a large spire howling, as he stared at it its gaze turned on him. Connar spun round to warn Mel and Howard but they had both disappeared leaving him alone, the howl came again but this time it was closer, he started to run, heading back to his bedroom door but as he pushed through it he found himself in a farm house. Confused he turned and locked the door before looking for a weapon to defend himself with. But now he had an overwhelming feeling that he had been here before and had gone through the exact same events, he lurched forward scrambling under the kitchen table taking hold of the iron poker he found lying under it. The first BANG came on the door and the frame instantly shuddered and bent, then the next BANG.

As it came he was wakened by a loud bang on his door. Startled, he bolted up. Sitting there not quite fully conscious, clutching the bed covers, he prepared to defend himself.

'Connar, you in there?'

Connar recognised Howard's voice, and almost laughed at his unfounded fear. He must have been dreaming about the werewolf.

'Yeah man, give me a minute, I'm just getting up.'

'Come on!' Howard yelled, "It's after seven. We're all starving.'

Connar's brain was still foggy. 'Okay okay,' he shouted back. 'Gimme a god-damn minute. I'll meet you down there.'

Silence followed, but only for a few seconds.

'Sure, take your time. See you later, dude.'

Dragging himself out of the soft, warm bed that he really didn't want to leave, Connar dressed quickly and headed down to the bar to join his team. They had taken up position close to the fire, which was now roaring like a furnace. The bar had filled up with locals and others from nearby villages and farms, and the American interlopers were drawing a lot of attention. Trekking the world and staying in the often remote places where their stories originated, they always seemed to attract the unwelcome interest of the locals. Some tried to take advantage of them by offering to be a guide, or by claiming to be a witness to whatever they had come to investigate. Whilst in the early days they had been taken for fools and had parted with considerable amounts of money for "inside information," they had soon grown wise to false story-tellers, and had learned to ignore the likely frauds.

Howard, as always, insisted on trying the local cuisine, and had Welch Cawl, after enquiring if Welsh Rarebit was indeed Rabbit, to which the barman had looked at him as if he were mad, and had shaken his head. The Welsh Cawl – a stew made with bacon, lamb, cabbage and leeks – arrived in a bowl, with a spoon. Rather a humble meal for Howard's refined taste. He had, however, ordered a large glass of the best Claret to accompany his meal. The others settled for a burger and fries, and a beer.

After their meal they relaxed and enjoyed the warmth of the fire as they started to discuss the present case.

Connar leaned towards the group. 'I read Ruby's research on the plane. Did any of you know that London Zoo had been involved in this?'

Each of them shook their heads.

Phil said, 'How did they get involved? Did they find anything?'

'No,' Connar said. 'They gave the farmer steel bear traps big enough for Grislys, but one of them got ripped open from the inside.'

Mel's tone seemed to reflect the concerned look on all their faces.

'What could have done that around here? Do they have bears here?'

Connar smiled. 'No, they haven't had bears here since the Mesolithic period, but something did wreck the cage.' He leaned back in his chair, prepared for a long discussion.

As the night moved along the fire died slowly until only a few smouldering embers remained, and the locals left one by one. Mel and Howard said goodnight, and left the bar. Connar, Ruby and Phil continued talking long into the night. As the clock approached midnight Phil stood up to leave.

'Do you have the car keys with you? I think I've left my bag in there.'

Connar fidgeted in his seat, checking his pockets before producing the single key he had been handed at the airport. Phil took it and headed for the door. As he reached for the handle the barman caught his attention.

'You don't want to go out there lad. I've locked us in for the night.'

Phil let go of the handle and turned to the short portly man who had welcomed them earlier that day. 'But I've left my things in the car. I need to get my stuff.'

The barman looked at him for a few seconds, and Phil could see he was considering the situation carefully.

'The door's locked now, I can't have people walking in and out all night. This is my inn, you see – my property. You'll be all right till the morning I'm sure, lad. Sit down and I'll bring you all a night cap, on the house.'

Phil was ready to stand his ground; he couldn't understand the objection to him going out for a moment, but as he was about to demand that he be allowed to retrieve his bag from the car, Ruby said,

'Philip, do as the man says. Come on, sit back down and enjoy a night cap.' She looked at him and gestured with her expression for him to return to his seat. She then turned and smiled at the inn keeper before returning her gaze to

Connar, and smirking.

Phil did as Ruby told him, but not without mumbling his protests.

The inn keeper brought four small whisky glasses with a generous measure in each of them. Handing over three of them, he held onto the last one for himself before sitting down in one of the empty chairs. 'So,' he began, 'what brings you Americans to our small village then?'

Connar looked at Phil and then back to Ruby before he leant across the table to reply.

'I don't believe I introduced my team earlier. This is Ruby, and Philip.'

'I'm Evan,' the inn keeper said. 'I've lived here all my life, born and bred. So, like I said, what brings you here?'

Ruby said, 'Nice to meet you Evan. We run a TV show in the states called *Myth Seekers*. You may have heard of it?'

'Yes, I've seen it. Recognised most of you as soon as you arrived.'

'Well,' Ruby continued, 'we heard about your wolf - the werewolf, or whatever, and we've come to investigate it - see if we can find any evidence.'

As the last word left Ruby's mouth Connar and Phil noticed an immediate change in Evan's expression. It had gone from jovial to one of alarm and then anger. His final expression made Ruby feel very uncomfortable. He placed his empty glass down on the table slowly and stared at it while he sighed heavily.

'I thought as much,' he said, his old green eyes now glaring at Connar. 'You listen here lad... I assume you're the boss?'

Connar nodded hesitantly, and Evan continued, now glaring at all three.

'There's nothing to be found here, it's just a story, you see, put about to keep the tourists out - stop them from camping and parking their bloody caravans all around our valley.'

Ruby said, 'Look, I know this is your patch – your part of the world, and I'm sure you know much more about it than we do. But our research tells a different story. For example, what about London Zoo's involvement? Doesn't that prove there was something strange or unexplained going on?'

Evan said, "It's just a story, nothing more. As for those English twpsyn that came with their fancy cages and traps...'

'Tw...p..sy?'

As Ruby struggled to pronounce the word Evan cut across her.

'Idiots! English idiots! Those zoo people will chase shadows if there's a chance to get their names in some science magazine.'

Phil said, 'But what about the cage being smashed open? And the tracks?'

Evan stood up and leaned across the table, his eyes focused hard on each of them. 'Now listen here. There'll be no good comes of roaming around the hills at night, especially at this time of year. Too many people have died in the dark, walking off edges they can't see. Now I'm warning you all – tomorrow, get in your car and leave. Fly back to where you came from and forget the whole damn thing. No good will come of it.'

With that, he left, muttering, 'No good will come of it, I tell you.'

Connar, Ruby and Phil sat still and silent, until Connar finally spoke.

'You think we hit a nerve?'

Ruby smiled a cautious, worried smile, and for the first time Connar saw a hint of fear in her stance.

'I think he's crazy,' Phil said. 'But do you think we oughta listen to him?'

Connar looked at Ruby.

She shook her head and sighed as she said, 'No, I don't think so. It's late. I'm tired, and being scared by a creepy old man in a creepy old hotel will seem as stupid as it is, in the morning. I'm going to bed.'

'Me too,' Phil said.

Connar nodded, and followed his friends upstairs.

4

The following morning Connar and Ruby sat in silence whilst they helped themselves to the traditional breakfast; neither of them wishing to speak about what had happened the previous night, or the warnings they'd been given. Though Evan's words had stayed with Ruby in her dreams and through to the bright sunlit morning, and whilst she had been sure last night that things wouldn't appear as unnerving in daylight, Evan's cautions gave her a feeling of foreboding that would stay with her all day. As they ate, Mel, Howard and Phil joined them at the table.

'Did you enjoy your late night?' Howard asked as he buttered his toast.

Ruby, Connar and Phil looked at each other before Connar replied,

'Hmm, it was... eventful.'

Howard said, 'What's up, Rubes?' She looked somewhat unsettled now.

She didn't look up from her cereal as she spoke. 'Oh, just Evan rambling on last night. It kinda made me uneasy. It's nothing, just a stupid old man thinking he can get one over on the outsiders.'

'Evan?'

'Yeah, you know, the bar tender, who is actually the owner.'

'What did he say?'

'Not much, really,' Connar answered. 'He was okay till we told him our plans, and then he went all Deliverance on us.'

'Saying what?'

'He said we should go home. That we shouldn't take notice of stupid stories, and that.......let me think...oh yeah, he said...' Connar put on his best Welsh accent. *'No good will come of it, I tell you!'*

They all sniggered like a bunch of naughty school children.

After finishing their breakfast Mel, Phil and Ruby went back to their rooms to collect their belongings and equipment, while Connar and Howard went back to the bar to pay for their rooms and breakfast.

'Evan?' Connar addressed the old man politely and with a smile, while Evan stood with his back to him, attending to the shelves. But as Connar expected, he didn't receive the same courtesy.

Without turning to face them Evan replied, 'No need for *your* money here. Just leave, and if you make it back down that hill, don't come back here.'

Connar placed the exact amount for their bill on the top of the bar. 'Take it, or leave it there, to be honest I don't care. And when we make it back home we'll be sure to put an accurate review on our show.'

Howard nodded in agreement, and both men walked away secure in the knowledge of their little victory over the local Evan. But the encounter sent a chill through both of them as they heard him say,

'You'll never see the United States again boys, mark my words.'

Outside in the warmth of the day the village and surrounding mountains looked so beautiful, that neither of them could believe that any danger could possibly live here. Surly in a place as picturesque as this, no-one could come to any harm? Connar lifted the tailgate for Ruby, Mel and Phil to load their bags with all they would need to disprove the wolf legend. They'd been unable to prove all the other tales they had chased on the show. Now angered somewhat, in his mind Connar had a goal - he was determined that following the warnings they'd received, he would do a first for the show: He would set out to completely disprove the Welsh Werewolf.

With the car packed they left The Old Inn and headed into the stunning countryside. It was early - just after 8am. - but the early start meant they'd have plenty of time to set up camp, and all of their equipment including the remote cameras and sensors. As they drove along, the public roads became narrower with every mile, until they found themselves travelling on a single track road. The stunning views they had enjoyed from the village seemed to transform slowly but noticeably to a backdrop of desolation and isolation. Even the sky seemed to lose the welcoming deep blue they had smiled at while loading the car. Now it appeared heavy and low; dull white with dapples of grey and black. Connar turned off the single track road onto a grass track marked *Public Access and Walkway*. He trundled the Galaxy slowly over the uneven ground, sometimes slipping the wheels into the larger tracks no doubt left by much larger 4x4's. He was starting to wish that Ruby had hired a four-wheel drive vehicle. After what seemed like an endless ride of jolts and bumps, Ruby put her hand on Connar's left arm and told him to stop. He applied the brakes softly and the car came to a halt, apparently in the middle of no-where.

Ruby said, 'Turn right, through those bushes.'

Connar looked to his right. 'Turn right *where* exactly?'

'Through those bushes,' she repeated. 'Trust me, the track's on the other side. It's where we need to be so that we won't be disturbed.'

Connar did not look convinced. 'You sure, Ruby? If we get stuck here, by the time we get help it'll be time to go home.'

'I'm sure. Go!' She urged him, waving her hand up and down as if dismissing him.

'Okay, you're the navigator!'

Connar pulled the wheel round and moved

the Galaxy forward and into the thicket of bushes now in front of them. As the nose of the car pushed through, they each clenched their teeth and drew in air as the thorns and thick stems scraped against the metal work of the car.

'Oh shit, that's gonna scratch," Howard said, as the car burst through and cleared the thicket.

Now they faced another green lane; this one heading up and away from the tourist routes.

'Smart ass,' Connar called Ruby.

She didn't reply. She just grinned smugly while looking ahead.

They followed the lane for another 7 miles until the Galaxy simply wouldn't go any further. But it had done well. It had managed to get much further than they had initially thought, largely because it had not rained here for weeks and the grass track was as hard as tarmac. Also partly because Connar enjoyed Green laning back home and knew how to keep the car moving on such terrain. Connar put the parking brake on then switched the engine off. Instantly the purr of the engine and the soft hiss of the air conditioning ceased, and the dashboard became blank as the courtesy lights illuminated the interior. This was it. Time to go.

They unpacked the car and left it there. Out here in the wilderness the modern, metallic-silver car looked as out of place as a horse and cart would do in the centre of a modern metropolis. Connar locked the vehicle and put the keys in the side pocket of his blue combat-style pants.

'Okay everybody, remember where we parked!' Mel joked as they headed away from the car.

Ruby replied with her usual lack of subtlety. 'You may laugh, but this lane isn't on any mass-produced map or GPS, so it would easily get lost out here.'

As 11am. approached they reached the designated base camp area, and like a well oiled machine each of them sprang into action managing their own part of the base set up. It was just turning 3:45pm by the time the base was up and operational. The team knew that sundown was around 9pm. at this time of year, which gave Howard, Phil and Mel time to travel out in an arc shaped formation to put the night vision equipment in place.

Connar and Ruby lit the stove inside the main tent - a large, blue, eight-berth tent with a living room and designated kitchen area. It also had 6 sleeping compartments: two doubles and four singles. As they heated the ready-made pasta meals, Howard, Phil and Mel returned.

'All set up and working, Boss,' Howard informed Connar as he walked into the tent.

'Thanks guys,' Connar said. 'Our mission over the next two nights is to prove once and for all that nothing more menacing than sheep is stalking this countryside. I'll show him. Him and his friggin' warnings!' He was about to continue his rant but Ruby interrupted him.

'Food's ready,' she said.

As the sun started its slow decent over the hills, the glow of their large camp fire became their only real source of light. The small solar powered and halogen battery lights placed around the base camp, didn't help much. The soft green glow of the night vision camera monitors were in direct contrast to the harsh blue light of the FLIR monitor. Connar and Phil planned the night-filming shots before heading out to test the hand-held night vision cameras. Ruby, Howard and Mel stayed behind, checking the four monitors.

The large metal stand that held the four 20" LCD monitors stood just inside the main blue tent. From this control unit they could see and control what each of the four remote cameras were looking at. Cameras 1, 2 and 3 were set in an arc, curving away from the camp site in a convex formation, with Camera 2 set up furthest from the camp at the top edge of the arc. This camera looked across a field and down onto the farm where the legend was said to have started. Camera 4 was the crowning jewel in Howard's range of precious equipment, with remote panning, zooming and ultra low light abilities. There wasn't much that Camera 4 wouldn't be able to capture, should the opportunity present itself. This special camera was set 100 meters out on its own.

After the briefing for tonight's shoot, Connar sat on a large log close to the fire, while Phil set his camera ready to record the opening part of the show. Ruby stood behind Phil and started the countdown, while Mel held the extended boom mike above his head.

Ruby said, 'Okay in 5, 4, 3,' and then followed the silent 2 and 1, and then she pointed at Connar.

'Hi! We're here in the mountains of Wales in the United Kingdom, and we're on a hunt for the Welsh Werewolf. Some locals have already tried to frighten us off these hills, warning us that our quest will end in terror, but as you know, that only makes it more exciting. Yes, this is gonna be a special show, and a little different from our usual format. Instead of trying to *find* the Welsh Werewolf, we're going to try to prove once and for all that this creature doesn't exist. It is said to have roamed these hills for over 300 hundred years, but we're hoping to reveal the truth behind the legend. Tonight Phil and I are gonna head out into the darkness, while my team stay here and monitor the cameras we set up earlier today. These include FLIR, night vision, digital still cameras with PIR sensors, and our new remote camera. So let's see what we can find, or rather, *can't* find.'

'And cut,' Ruby called. 'Looked okay to me but we better make sure. Play it back for me, Philip.'

Connar decided he was happy with the first shoot. He always maintained that he didn't want the show's presentation to be too glossy, so that it retained the raw "fly on the wall" feel that the earlier shows had achieved. 'Okay Phil, let's head out.'

Phil put on the mount that he always wore on mobile shoots - the light metal frame that sat snug on his shoulders, which carried a light and two small cameras. He held a night vision camera towards Connar's face, to capture his reactions to anything they might see. Finally, he set a forward viewing camera with a back light, on a band around Connar's head, to let the viewer see exactly what Connar saw. Phil picked up the larger, more powerful hand-held night vision camera, and both men set off in a north west direction, towards Camera 1 on the left edge of the arc formation. As they carefully pushed through the heavy undergrowth and thick mountain grasses, their cameras continued to film nothing but darkness, and Phil could see nothing but the green hazy static that the night vision camera produced as it peered through the blackness. The only sounds they heard were the whispers of the breeze and the static that hissed over the walkie talkies.

After an uneventful trudge of what seemed like hours but in fact was around 30 minutes, they reached camera 1 - mounted on its tripod, standing silently like a sentry guard, looking out into the absolute darkness that surrounded it.

'I guess we'd better do a piece to camera now, and report on... absolutely nothing at all,' Connar said, laughing.

Phil responded with a smile. 'I've got the camera on you, Connar, so in 5, 4, 3...' His right hand, just visible inside the limits of Connar's head light, gestured 2 and 1.

Connar's face illuminated green against the hazy background, and his eyes stood out as bright white. In his most sincere, professional tone, he quietly whispered,

'We've reached the first point on the trail and so far none of our equipment has picked up any movement or sound.'

Phil pressed the pause button. 'Isn't that a little strange?' he said.

'Isn't *what* a little strange?'

'What you just said. You said the cameras haven't picked up any movement or sound, and come to think of it, there's no sound at all. I mean, totally no sound.'

'Yeah, it's weird. I think we should check in - make sure the others are okay.' Connar fumbled for his walkie talkie, which was pinned to his jacket collar. 'Connar to base, come in, over.'

Static. Then, 'Base here. Go ahead Connar, over.' More static.

'Mel, you got any movement or sound around you? Over.'

The sound of static increased after every communication.

'That's a negative, Connar. Nothing to report here. All quiet, over.'

'Base, I mean any sounds at all. *Anything*, Mel? Over.'

The radio hissed and crackled so much, it hurt Connar's ears.

'No, Connar, nothing at all. No sound of anything. You?'

'No. We're gonna check out Camera 2 now. Stay focused, you guys. Over.'

'Will do, base over and out.'

Connar had to remove his ear piece for a moment, to let his ear recover from the rush of static that had almost deafened him.

Pushing through the darkness again, with only the dim beam of Connar's forward pointing light and Phil's night vision camera to guide them, they eventually reached the next camera at the head of the arc. Perched securely on its stand, it too stared out into the dead of the night that seemed to stretch on endlessly.

Phil said, 'Look, everything seems okay here. Why don't we call this a successful test run for the first night, and head back to camp? This place has an eerie feel to it.'

Connar looked around him, panning the small white light on his head in a 360 degree loop, and considered the situation carefully before he answered. They hadn't been out for as long as they'd planned, but the atmosphere around them was getting denser and colder. 'Yeah, I think you're right. Base are getting a feed from the other cameras, we don't need to be out here right now. We'll head back and shoot some filler there.'

The walk back took some time; the terrain difficult enough during the day with the correct walking shoes and gear, but at night with the temperature falling fast, and carrying equipment, it took them twice as long to cover the same ground. Eventually, following their GPS, they caught sight of the glow from the fire, and as they drew closer they saw the soft lights that hung around the tents.

As they approached Ruby stepped out of the tent to welcome them back.

'You know, since you asked us about any sounds we've really paid attention and you're right, there are no sounds at all, not even sheep. I guess out here sound should carry for miles.'

Howard and Mel had joined them as they stood by the edge of the fire.

'Of course, you know why it's normally like this, don't you?' Howard said in a confident tone.

'No, why?' Mel asked him.

Ruby cut Howard off before he had the chance to shine with his Discovery Channel knowledge. 'Predators. Normally when it's quiet like this, there's an apex predator around, and anything with any sense hides or leaves.'

Mel looked nervously between Ruby and Howard, then said, 'Shouldn't we hide or leave, if that's true?'

They all looked at Connar for guidance.

He ran his hands through his hair while he thought about it. 'I don't think we're in any danger. I'm not sure Wales has a large nocturnal eco system, and besides, if the sheep haven't been taken in by the farmers they'll probably be fast asleep, which is where I should be. And going by how your over-active imaginations are getting to you, I think you oughta be in bed too.'

With that, Connar headed into the tent. 'Howard, are the cameras set to record if anything passes in front of them?' he called back.

'Yes,' he replied as he sat at the monitoring station.

'Then I suggest we all get some sleep and let the tech take the night shift.'

It was 9:00am when they regrouped for breakfast. Howard had been the first to wake up, and had spent the early morning scanning through the footage that the remote cameras had taken during the night. They hadn't captured anything unusual - in fact they hadn't captured anything at all - and given that the arc formation of the cameras covered a visible area of two square miles, they should have seen some form of wild life, if only a small rodent. He brought up his findings and his uneasy feeling about this, over breakfast. The group discussed it in depth, and they all decided that it was nothing more than a strange coincidence. They had all been on too many shoots and heard too many tall tales, to be scared off by blank screens and lack of evidence. They were all with Connar now in proving the grumpy inn keeper wrong.

Connar decided they would extend the filming today, to look for any signs of the animals normally found in these parts.

He asked Phil, 'Can you set up the portable camera again? We'll take that out into the field today and look for any tracks or signs that anything lives up here.'

'Sure, Connar.'

Phil headed over to the table where he'd left the camera, pulled up a chair and began to review the footage he had taken the previous night.

Connar then turned to Howard and Mel. 'Can you two go out and check the still cameras you strapped to the trees yesterday? See if they caught anything passing by.' He then turned to Ruby and discreetly gestured her to follow him outside.

She walked with Connar over to the remnants of the fire. All that remained now were the grey ashes of the burnt logs, and a large patch of brown earth inside the pit they had dug and surrounded with rocks.

'You okay, Connar?' It was the first time she had seen him look worried or scared, since they had started this show. Of all the mysteries and legends they had investigated, this one seemed to have got to him.

He stood with his foot resting on a rock, leaning on his raised leg. 'What do you think of this one?' he asked her.

'I think......" she hesitated before continuing. 'I think it's like the rest of them - a story that's carried on for generations, to pull in the tourists and feed the local community. Like all these legends do. I mean, look at Loch Ness or Bigfoot, and all the businesses and stores that have sprung up around the areas of supposed sightings. It's no wonder the locals keep them going! That's what I think. How about you?'

Connar shifted on the spot, pushing his foot into the grey ash and moving it around, but at the same time avoiding eye contact with Ruby. Eventually he sighed, and answered, 'Well, it seems to me that there's some real history to this case. I mean, there's the research you gave me on the plane, and old Evan back at the hotel...'

'Evan! That senile old fool! What he said was

bullshit, Connar.'

'It's not *what* he said, it's the way he said it. You saw the look on his face when I told him our plans. That wasn't put on for the tourists, that was genuine fear. And it's not just him. Look around - there's nothing, not even in daylight. Where are the birds? Cattle? Or even the sheep? Christ, Ruby, have you stood in any sheep shit yet? Or cow shit? Because I know I haven't, and by now we should all have stood in some foul smelling green crap of sorts!'

His voice was raised now, and Ruby could see he was genuinely caught up in this myth; this legend. She reached out and took his hand.

'Connar listen to me. Okay there may be something up here - a big cat or even a wolf. But just over that ridge sheep and cows will be shitting everywhere. You wanna step in shit, just go over there.'

She smiled to reassure him, and Connar forced a brief laugh.

'Look,' she continued, 'we're here for one more night then we'll pack up and get the fuck outa here. We'll jump on a plane back home and then show this place for what it is. Then I promise I'll find a totally fake-looking UFO for us to investigate, okay?'

He smiled down at her and let go of her hand. Just as he was about to thank her for the reassurance, Phil burst out of the tent and called to them.

'What's so urgent, Philip?' Ruby asked as she rushed towards him.

Phil replied with only word. 'Watch.'

When Ruby and Connar were at his side he pressed the play button on his camera. The screen flickered to life and a green grainy image of Connar doing his piece to camera, came up.

'Okay, so that's the piece I did last night,' Connar said.

Phil slammed the stop button and pressed rewind. The normally laid back cameraman was agitated. 'Watch again,' he urged, and this time he played it back in slow motion. The picture was a little distorted but watch-able. 'Watch carefully as you're talking... keep watching.'

On screen, Connar's mouth moved slowly up and down as the frames passed one by one, and then Phil pushed *pause*. As the image froze he pointed to the area just behind Connar's right ear. Ruby and Connar closed in on the small screen, screwing their faces up as they tried to focus on what Phil was attempting to show them. As their eyes unscrambled the distorted image it became clear to see that, passing behind Connar as he talked to the camera, was a large black mass with what appeared to be a head. It turned to face the camera for a split second, and in the white-ish green of the grainy image, its illuminated eyes seemed to exude evil itself.

5

Connar's hand shot to his mouth as he gasped. He turned to look at Phil. 'What the fuck was that?'

Phil simply shook his head.

Ruby's reaction followed Connar's seconds later, with an audible draw of breath. She was clearly shaken and turned ashen white, as beads of sweat formed on her brow. She sat down and leaned forward, resting her hands on her knees and letting her head fall forward as she took deep slow breaths. Connar asked Phil to replay the tape and stop as the black mass came into view.

He pointed at the image. 'What could that be, Phil?'

Phil shrugged his shoulders. 'I'm not sure. Maybe a large cat or dog.'

Ruby immediately snapped back at him, 'You know that's not a fucking cat or dog, Philip!'

Phil stood up and turned to face her. 'And what do you think it is, Ruby? A sheep? Or maybe it's an overgrown rabbit, or - let me guess - a werewolf!'

Ruby had never seen Philip so bold.

'Why not, Philip? It could be anything. Connar said himself there's a lot of evidence for this case, and then there's the lack of anything else going on.' She looked at Connar for support.

In a flash a thousand thoughts whizzed through his mind, but one kept pushing its way back to the front and Connar went into full sales pitch mode. He knew he'd have the last word - this was his show; his baby, and the network trusted him - but he also knew he had to have his team on board. 'Look, I don't know what that was for sure, it could have been a large cat or dog, maybe a Badger. It could have been a fox - hell it could even be the damn werewolf! But what I do *know* is that we have a chance here, finally, to find proof of something and perhaps capture it on tape for the world to see. C'mon guys, you know I'm right.'

Phil nodded, but Phil was easy - Connar knew he would fall into line. It was Ruby he needed to win over, and by the look on her face she was far from convinced. But he continued anyway.

'What do you say Ruby? We could make history here - be famous the world over.'

'We *are* famous the world over. And what about proving Evan wrong and ruining his tourist trade?'

Connar's expression changed from hopeful to frustrated. 'Fuck him, I don't give a shit. If we prove this thing is real and capture it on VT or audio, or both, we can buy the fucking Inn from him!'

Ruby felt pressured and it showed.

Connar softened his tone. 'Ruby, you said yourself that just over the hill there would be cattle and sheep and plenty of shit too! And I promise next time we'll investigate the worst-looking, most fake-like, shittiest UFO tape we can find.'

He smiled at her, and he could tell by her expression that he had won her over with his charm and persuasion. He held his arms out, palms up like a child faking innocence. 'Ruby, come one, you know I'm right.'

'Okay. But there are rules. No-one leaves the camp tonight - we have all the remote cameras we need. And tomorrow, evidence or not, we pack up and leave first light. I want to be back on a damn plane tomorrow night without fail. Am I clear?'

Connar nodded, then gave her a hug. 'I knew you'd come round.'

He gave Phil the thumbs up sign.

Howard and Mel reached the first of the digital still cameras they had set up near the closest river to their camp. This was always standard practice no matter what animal or legend they had been challenged to find - at some point it would have to drink. Howard clicked open the card reader cover and slid the small 1GB SD card out of the slot, and plugged it into the side of his phone. He selected the folder and clicked open, but as with the video cameras in the arc, the camera had not been tripped by any movement and the card was still empty.

'Shit," he muttered, as he slid it back into the camera and closed the waterproof cover. 'Let's go to the next one, Mel.'

'Nothing on that one?' she asked, as they followed the river down stream.

Howard shook his head. 'Uh uh. Zilch.'

The trail along the side of the river was uneven and the ground damp, and so they had trouble keeping pace as well as their balance, as they pushed on.

The second camera also showed nothing. Howard pushed his hand under his baseball cap and scratched his head. 'I don't understand. Not even a deer or a vole or a beaver... if they have beavers here. You know, Mel, there oughta be something moving around, if not at night then at least during the day. This is the only fresh water source for miles.'

As they headed towards the next camera, the trail was so narrow and the river's banks so steep, that they couldn't walk side by side. Mel meandered slowly behind Howard, losing enthusiasm for their task. As they approached the site of the third camera the trees on the river banks closed over them, diffusing what little sunlight that had managed to penetrate the heavy grey clouds. The trees were so low that Howard felt he could reach up and touch them. Mel felt closed in by them, as if she were inside a sealed plastic bubble.

When Howard reached the third camera, he

yelled, "Mel! Come here, quick!' He waved his hand, ushering her to run faster. 'Look at this,' he said as she arrived at his side.

He pointed to the ground, where the camera lay crushed; the case open and the plastic tie strap they had used to fasten it to the tree, slashed and lying next to it. Mel moved her gaze up from the ground to the tree, and what she saw there troubled her more then the sight of the camera: Across the tree trunk at the height where the camera had been, were deep slashes in the bark. Four slashes running parallel in a diagonal direction. She could tell that this had been one fast continuous strike.

She placed her hands on the deep cuts, pushing her finger tips along them. The lacerations were two inches deep, and she had to spread her hand as wide as she could to match the strike pattern with her own fingers.

Howard moved in for a closer look, and put his own fingers in the grooves. 'What the fuck.... What the hell could have done this out here?'

Mel shrugged her shoulders. 'If we'd been in North America I'd have said a larger than normal Brown Bear. But we're in Wales, and like Connar said, the last bears here died out thousands of years ago. So I have no idea.'

Howard felt a sinking feeling in the pit of his stomach. His hand fell away from the tree and he bent down to pick up the remains of the camera.

'Is that any good?' Mel asked.

'It could be. So long as the SD card isn't damaged we may see something.'

Mel laughed nervously. 'But do we want to?'

'I'm not so sure about that!' Howard checked his watch. 'Come on, we'll go check the last camera.'

He didn't want to go. It was the first time since joining the show, that he'd had a feeling of dread. Most of the investigations followed fruit loops, as he called them - just people wanting some publicity, or some proof because they really did believe the stories they'd been told as a child. But he instinctively knew that this one was different.

The walk to the last camera was at a faster pace than the first three. Even so, by the time they reached it, it was already 5pm. This camera was still intact and strapped securely to the tree, and like the first two, it showed nothing on its memory card.

'That's it for me,' Howard said, as he clipped the card back in and slid the cover over it. 'Let's head back to camp. It'll only take thirty minutes if we hurry.'

'Yeah, let's go,' Mel agreed, eager to get back. She didn't want to spend any more time than she had to, out in the open.

Back at the camp Phil was checking and double checking the equipment, including his new Sony camera - or "Camera 4" - designated as such because it had been plugged into the fourth and last monitor on the stand.

'Is everything okay, Phil?' Connar asked, as he came back into the tent.

'Everything's cool. All remote cameras are A okay and Camera 4 is responding to the remote control. We can look pretty much anywhere and in any weather condition.'

'That's good, we gotta keep our eyes open tonight.'

'What about the FLIR and infra-red cameras?'

'We'll operate them by hand as usual, but just from inside the camp tonight. I'm not taking any risks.'

'So you think that *was* something?' Phil asked.

'I don't know. But if it's a big cat or a large dog I don't wanna meet it again. Just because it walked past us last night doesn't mean it will do the same thing tonight.'

Phil nodded. He knew Connar was right. From the camp they could pretty much do all they needed to do, and besides, after checking the weather forecast for tonight the cloud base should disperse, leaving a clear night. They would have the starlight and moonlight to help them.

Connar went outside to talk to Ruby, who was clearing the ashes from the previous night's fire so that she could light a new one.

'Can I get your thoughts on this, Ruby?' he asked as he approached her from behind.

She didn't turn round, intent on building the largest fire possible, even if it meant burning some of their stuff. 'I've made my thoughts clear, Connar. Whatever happens tonight, we leave at first light tomorrow.'

He stood beside her, absent-mindedly pushing the ash around with his right foot as he looked ahead. The clouded sky seemed to stretch forever, casting fleeting dark shadows across the landscape and over the hills, as black clouds were hastened along by the strengthening wind.

Ruby finished building the new fire, which she hoped would keep the black mass that had shown up on screen with Connar, out of their camp. She lit the paper under the kindle wood - which was piled on top of the logs they had brought with them, which were on top of the wood scavenged from the local area - and stood back to watch the flames take hold. By the time Mel and Howard returned, the fire was roaring high into the darkening night sky. Red cinders flew up and floated gently back down, extinguishing before they hit the damp moor ground. Connar stood in front of the fire, warming his hands.

'Christ Connar,' Howard said as he approached, 'that's a hell of a fire you have going there.'

'Not my doing. We have Ruby to thank for this one. Before you stop for a heat, I have something I need to show you.'

Inside the tent Phil and Ruby were looking intently at the four large monitors.

Connar said, 'Phil, can you show Mel and Howard the footage?'

'Yeah, sure. Pull up a chair, guys.' Phil spun his chair around and got the camera in position. 'Look carefully,' he instructed, then he pushed the play button. As Mel and Howard watched the large black mass come into view behind Connar, both pulled back and gasped with surprise.

Howard immediately reached into his jeans pocket, and showed Phil the memory card he had pulled from the smashed still camera. 'We found this by the third digital camera, or what was left of it.'

Connar moved in for a closer look. 'What do you mean, what was left of it?'

Mel said, 'It was in pieces, Connar. Smashed up on the ground, and the tie strap had been slashed. Also, the tree trunk had deep cuts in it.'

Phil slotted the memory card into the side of the laptop they had been watching, and clicked on the icon for "Image 0001."

On seeing the picture, Mel covered her mouth, while Howard put his hands on top of his head and squeezed them into fists. Phil just stared, in disbelief. Connar didn't know what to do.

'No! *I don't believe it!*' Ruby yelled. She backed

away from the image, repeating, 'It can't be, it just can't be!'

Connar approached her to try and calm her. This was so unlike Ruby. Taking a soft hold of her arm, he turned her away from the screen and lead her out of the tent.

With the immediate shock of the image gone, Phil pulled himself back towards the laptop and leaned into the screen; his inquisitive nature prevailing once more. He needed to understand the image, but he couldn't make sense of it. Nothing he had ever seen before resembled this image. He didn't know such a thing even existed.

'What could it be, Phil?' Mel asked.

'I really don't know. I think what's here is a CGI creation straight out of Hollywood. I mean, nothing like this exists, does it? But then, with the other footage and the other odd things we've noticed, I can't actually say that. What do I think it is? Honestly, I think it's our werewolf.'

He got up and went outside, leaving the image on the screen. Howard and Mel looked at it again. It was obvious now, that the camera had captured a blurred image. The thing must have been passing quickly when the sensor caught it and the flash illuminated. Even so, the beast's head was fairly clear - its large skull with bright, deep set eyes, large erect ears, and a long snout with canine teeth jutting out from the curling lips. They followed the outline down to where the image ended at the base of the skull, and could just see the tops of its shoulders covered in thick matted grey hair.

Howard and Mel looked at each other. No words were needed.

They joined the others outside.

The others stood around the fire, talking loudly and gesturing in all directions as Howard and Mel approached them. Howard could tell that an argument was breaking out, and as usual Ruby was at the centre of it, her voice carrying the furthest.

'No way, Connar!' she snapped, 'You've just seen that picture. Along with the video, you must see that it's not safe here. We have to leave; get back to the car.'

Connar tried to reason with her. 'Ruby, there isn't time. It's almost dark now. By the time we pack up and walk back to the car, even if we're able to find it in the dark, I doubt I could get back along the green lanes.'

'You managed it when we got here.'

'Yes, during the day when I could navigate and straddle the ruts and ditches, but even high beams wont give me enough visibility. We've gotta stay here tonight. Whatever's out there didn't bother us last night.'

'Didn't *bother* us? It damn near walked into you!' She threw her arms into the air in sheer frustration.

Phil dared to speak next. 'It didn't nearly walk

into us, Ruby, it looked directly at me. It knew where we were, it saw us clearly.'

Connar's face dropped. 'You had to say that, didn't you?'

'Yeah, fucking great, Philip,' Ruby snarled. 'Now you're telling me the fucking thing can see in the dark! Anything else I should know? Like, can it hear us from four miles away?'

Now Howard spoke up. 'It could hear you, Rubes.'

All of them - including Mel, who had stood quietly at the back – looked at Howard. It was the first time any of them had heard him join an argument and shout down Ruby, but apparently he wasn't phased by the ordeal. He continued making his point.

'Listen everyone, if it is a large cat or dog, or even a werewolf, one thing's for sure - it will have excellent hearing and excellent night vision, and as with all predators or hunters, it will also have an acute sense of smell. But we have the intelligence and equipment to even the odds. Our remote night vision cameras are standing guard for us. Anything that moves towards this camp from any direction will be seen long before it can get here. If it is a large dog or cat, it'll avoid contact with humans. The night will probably pass without incident, and tomorrow we can pack up and drive out.'

He walked away and sat on one of the camping chairs placed around the fire. The others followed in silence.

For a while no-one spoke. The only sound was the crackle of burning wood as the fire blazed on.

Eventually Connar broke the uncomfortable silence. 'Hey Phil, what's your best guess as to what we've captured on camera?'

Phil hesitated before giving his honest answer. 'Like I said to Mel and Howard, I'd say it's our werewolf. It's gotta be – it doesn't actually resemble a big cat, which is the only other thing that could have made those deep scratches in the tree trunk, apart from a bear, of which there are zero in this vicinity. I guess he was startled when the camera went off, and he attacked the source of the light. Jeez, I can't believe I'm saying this. A *werewolf*? You know, maybe it's an overgrown wild dog. It kinda looks like a dog, I guess.'

'Are you saying it's a dog or a werewolf?' Howard asked.

'I dunno, what do *you* think it is, wise guy? Why do I have to be the one who pins a name badge on it? I'm a cameraman, not a fucking wildlife expert.'

'Back in the tent you seemed pretty sure.'

'I'm not sure, I just thought it *could* be the werewolf. Maybe I just want one of these trips to turn out to be genuine, you know?'

The silence returned. This time caused by a Mexican Wave of guilt, as each stood to defend his or her integrity. It was Connar who said what everyone felt.

'Look, we always go into these cases with an open mind. We never set out to make a fool of anyone. We give their stories a fair shot, and only after a proper investigation, do we say that there's no proof. We don't say it isn't real - we just say we can't prove it. Plus, we do a damned good job at entertaining the folks with this stuff. Every case is genuine – a genuine mystery worth solving.'

'But we never solve them,' Mel added.

Ruby said, 'So we cheated for once and tried to get clever. So what? Connar's right, we never do that. Okay this time we set out to disprove the theory, maybe that was a little sneaky...'

'Yeah, and now I think we're paying the price,' Mel said.

'It's not fair,' Connar said. 'The first time we do try to make a fool of someone, it backfires and gets thrown in our faces. I can hear that old guy now. *No good will come of it, I tell you.'* The Welsh accent had appeared automatically as he'd quoted Evan.

A shiver shot up Ruby's spine. 'I never thought we would find a true myth or living legend – I never believed in this crap. I wouldn't have gotten involved if I thought there was ever a chance of actually seeing something that's not supposed to exist. And now I'm camping in a fucking werewolf's back yard!' She turned and headed for the tent. 'I'll take first shift watching the monitors.'

'I've never seen her so spooked,' Mel whispered.

'Me neither,' Connar said, 'but I think this is real. This truly is a threat.'

'Yeah, this time we may have found what we're looking for,' Phil said. 'I'm gonna set up the infra-red - you know, check everything. Make sure we're safe.'

'I'll go with you buddy,' Howard said.

'Thanks. I'm sorry I snapped at you earlier.'

'Hey, no sweat. We're all getting a little spooked out here.'

Mel and Connar stood close together. As the sun finally vanished behind the hills they could feel the dark and cold encroach on them as if it were some malevolent force encircling them. The orange glow of the fire cast dancing shadows around the camp, like lively spirits bursting through from the afterlife then retreating after allowing only a glimpse of their existence. Beyond the camp site was dense, solid blackness. Connar and Mel retreated back to the tent guided only by their torches and the small camping lights, but between the circles of light they provided it was pitch black and nothing could be seen not even your own hand held inches from your face. Mel felt vulnerable as if each dark area was hiding a monster of its own. As they reached the tent Mel pushed her way through the canvas door and as Connar stepped through he turned to take one more look. As he gazed into the void of black he had a primeval feeling that something was staring back.

6

The atmosphere inside the tent was one of foreboding, fear, confusion and disbelief. As Ruby kept watch, the others compared previous myths they had investigated over the years. But even as they tried to evaluate their present situation, doubt and dread hung in the enclosed tent, like a dark mist shrouding them in its torment.

Howard and Mel took the next shift. They scanned the screens continually for the slightest of movement or change in the shadows. With the cameras in night vision mode, the eerie green view they provided made the shadows penetrable, and Howard and Mel could see into the darkest recesses of the dales. Both fought to keep their imaginations in check, to stop them from visualising all sorts of monstrous creatures leaping out at them.

Phil and Connar prepared to go outside with their FLIR and infra-red hand-held cameras, as these cameras could not be remotely controlled. Ruby had gone into her bedroom and zipped it shut, so hopefully she wouldn't know they were venturing out from the relative safety of the tent.

'Ready Phil?' Connar asked his nervous-looking friend.

'Not really, but I guess this has to be done.'

Phil pulled the zipper up and pointed the camera through the gap in the tent doorway. He directed it around the camp site, and Connar stood over his shoulder as they both watched at the 5inch screen. The camp site looked empty. Looking further afield, the surroundings showed up cold blue. The saw the black outlines of the now redundant tents they had used for storage, rest room and spare sleeping quarters, and then a large white hot plume as the fire came into view.

Phil looked round at Connar. 'I think we're clear to go.'

Connar nodded, and they crept outside. Mel fastened the zipper securely as soon as they'd left, still trying to convince herself that the beast was just a wildcat.

Outside the night air was clear and still. A large full moon illuminated the night sky, and the orange glow from the fire added to the light. Connar and Phil stood together in front of the fire, both reluctant to move away from its protection.

'Okay, you head over there,' Connar said, pointing to the right. He headed off slowly, to the left.

Philip moved away cautiously, slowly sweeping his camera from left to right as he went. When he passed the edge of the camp site, he stopped and panned through 360 degrees, but his screen showed nothing unusual - no heat sources or heat traces left by recent activity. On the other side of the camp Connar was doing the same; his infra-red camera only showing blacks and dark blues. No reds, yellows or oranges indicating a heat source. Every few seconds Connar looked up, away from the screen, fully expecting to see those eyes again, but he saw nothing other than absolute darkness. He felt as if he was in a void on the very edge of an abyss. Even though he knew that the moors stretched out before him, every footstep seemed to be a leap of faith – hoping that his foot would make contact with the ground and that he wouldn't step off the edge and fall into the blackness. He looked down at the screen. Still nothing showed, and so he advanced further out, guided by the white ghostly light of the full moon.

Back inside the tent Howard stared continuously at the monitors whilst Mel paced up and down, occasionally checking the screens and hoping there would be nothing to see. Each time she looked it became harder to look again, but she forced herself, and each time she breathed a sigh of relief when the screen showed nothing suspicious. Howard was still scanning the monitors. Cameras 1 to 3 showed nothing in their fixed lines of site. He turned his gaze to the last screen, and Camera 4. He picked up the remote unit and moved the small joystick to the left. In the pitch-black night, just outside of the camp, the camera started to move. Its images relayed instantly back to the screen. Pulling the joystick back, Howard panned the camera around, and the green grainy image showed him nothing but the moorlands. He hit the centre button on the remote, sighed, and rested his head in his hands. Outside the camera automatically centred itself staring dead once more; ahead into the pitch black.

His peaceful moment of respite was broken by the sudden shriek of Mel's screams. Startled, he spun round to look at her. She was pointing past him to the screens. He immediately spun back in his seat, turned back to come face to face with the display from Camera 4. In the fuzzy image of the night vision green, they saw it. The thing they could hardly believe existed. Staring at the camera, its large wolf-like face filled the screen; canine teeth hanging from its top lips, which were curled and pulled back. Howard followed its wrinkled snout, up to its eyes. He stared into them, stunned by their almost human appearance. He was transfixed, unable to move, and watched as it stood on its hind legs, then only its chest filled the screen. Howard knew that it must be around 7feet in height. He watched in fear as it turned and walked past the camera, towards the camp.

Connar had heard Mel's scream, faint in the distance behind him. Using the Infra-red camera as a guide, he turned and headed back to camp. He had wandered further than he'd intended, but as his camera had continued to show nothing, he'd pushed on and was now quite far from the camp. Moving as quickly as he could over the uneven ground - each step nothing more than a guess as to where the ground might be - he hurried back.

Phil was much closer; he hadn't ventured as far as Connar. Mel's scream seemed to split the air with a shrill sound that sent a sudden tingle of fear down his spine. Like Connar, he too turned and headed back, all the time fearful of what he may find. When he reached the camp he ran past the fire, towards the large tent. 'Open up.' he shouted as he got closer. The zipper was raised just high enough to allow him through. Inside he found Mel sitting in his editing chair, cradling her legs as if she were back in the womb. He looked at Howard, who was now pulling the tent zipper back down.

'What happened here?' he said, trying to catch his breath after running back.

Howard stood straight after securing the zipper. 'We saw it, it was on Camera 4.'

'Saw what?'

'What do you think? We saw the fucking werewolf, man! It was right there on the screen.'

'Did you record it?' Phil asked.

'What?' Howard was visibly calming down, now that Phil was there. 'Shit, I didn't think to record it. I mean, I saw it there on the screen, its face, its teeth, those eyes, they seemed… I dunno, so real, like human eyes, full of anger and...' He hesitated as he recalled the image. 'Full of death.' There was a tone of defeat and hopelessness in his voice now. He sat down in his chair, and turned back to the monitors.

Ruby burst through her bedroom door, still pulling on her sweatshirt over her pyjamas. Alarmed first by Mel's scream then by Howard's account of Camera 4's pictures, she was relieved to see that all was quiet now. Howard had returned to his chair and Philip just stood there, seemingly dumbfounded by the night's events.

Putting her personal fears aside and assuming her professional responsibility, she looked at the blank monitor and asked Howard, 'Which way did it head?'

Mel and Phil looked at Howard, wondering if he would tell Ruby the truth.

Howard looked at Ruby, and decided it would be disrespectful to lie to her. She seemed back in control; back to her cold, unapproachable self.

'Right this way,' he said. 'It's coming straight for us.'

They waited for someone to speak, each hoping that one of the others would have a plan - a strategy that would lead them safely out of danger. But none of them knew what to do.

Finally Ruby said, 'How far can that camera turn round?'

'360 degrees,' Howard said.

'Turn it round and point it towards us.'

Howard pushed the joystick to the left. Instantly the camera responded and started to turn on its mount. Howard watched the display, and when it reached 180 he let go of the stick, and the camera stopped.

Phil moved closer to the screen. 'Okay, now zoom in.'

'On what? Howard said. 'It's too dark, even with the night vision. It has its limits.'

'I know that!' Phil snapped at him. 'Just zoom in.'

Howard sighed heavily to register his complaint, and hit the remote zoom. The lens on the camera extended, sending its images back to them as it closed in on the camp. But as it reached its maximum capability the image became too grainy, and deteriorated beyond use. All they could make out with any certainty was the bright white blurred mass in the middle of the screen, which they knew was the camp fire. Howard zoomed back out a short distance until the fire came into focus as a small white moving shape in the middle of the screen.

'There, you see? Nothing! It's too damn dark to be of any use.'

'Yeah, you were right,' Phil conceded. 'But it

was worth a try.'

Static interrupted the short-lived silence.

'Is everyone okay? I heard a scream, over.'

It was Connar.

'Christ, *Connar!* He'll walk right into it!' Phil yelled. He grabbed his walkie talkie. 'Connar, come in, it's Phil, over.'

'Connar here. What happened? Over.'

'Listen to me real carefully - do *not* come back to camp, I repeat, do not come back to camp, over.'

More static.

'What? Why? What's going on there? Over.'

Connar slowed his advance towards camp, unsure of what to do. He moved his camera back and forth, frantically searching for anything that moved. A sense of panic came over him, and he fought to stay in control. He knew if it took hold, his chances of reaching safety would be dramatically reduced. His fear was rising all the time, convincing him that each step would bring him closer to the black mass caught on camera the previous night. Scanning the area with the camera, he could feel his heart thumping, trying to escape from his chest. His handset crackled again.

'We think it's close by,' Phil continued. ' Howard saw it on Camera 4, heading this way. Be careful, over.'

'What? You've seen it? It was definitely *it?* Over.'

Phil raised his voice, exasperated. 'Yes! I repeat, don't come back here. Be careful. Find somewhere to hide until I tell you the coast is...'
Tshhhhhhh.

Connar stopped dead in his tracks. The static was deafening, but he tried anyway. 'Phil? Over.'

Nothing.

'Phil! Come in, over.'

Still nothing.

He stood there in the dark, frozen to the spot. He didn't know what to do or where to turn. He spun around, half looking at the camera, half looking out into the void of the night.

He hit the side of his handset and whispered in a loud, frantic rasp, 'Phil, Howard, Mel....anyone there? Over.'

Tshhhhhh. Nothing but static.

'Shit *shit shit!*' He hadn't a clue what to do, cut off from everyone and everything.

Phil raised his voice, exasperated. 'Connar! I repeat, don't come back here. Be careful. Find somewhere to hide until I tell you the coast is...'
Tshhhhhhh.

The tent shook violently. Phil jumped, and dropped the walkie talkie. The shaking continued till the camp lights fell off the tent supports, smashing on the ground. Only one light, which was secured to the trusses, remained lit. It swung around at random, its

95

glow dancing over the canvas, creating alternate flashes of light and sudden veils of darkness. Phil searched in the fleeting bursts of light for the handset, but as he bent down to search the floor, the tent ripped and sagged, the light spun around like a search light then fell to a low level, and inside the tent became dark. Mel turned to flee, heading for the door. She pushed the sagging fabric to one side, grabbed the zipper tag, and started to lift it. She heard Ruby screaming in fear, behind her. Phil was still trying to locate his handset, and Howard was pushing up against the sagging roof, looking for a way out.

Mel looked back as she pulled the zipper up, and she called to Ruby.

'Come on, we gotta get outa here. Ruby…'

The dim light swung back, and once again Ruby was completely hidden from sight. Mel held the tent flaps open, waiting for the light to swing back on Ruby. When it did, she saw that Ruby was not alone. Standing behind her, towering over her, the creature's arms were raised above its massive head. Mel could make out its claws – long, razor-sharp claws.

She yelled again, 'Ruby!'

But as she called to her friend the light swung away and darkness covered her again. Mel stayed rooted to the spot. She had to know what had become of Ruby. It seemed like ages before the light swung back to her, but as it did the sight that met Mel's eyes filled her with more fear and horror than she thought possible. Ruby had been lifted from the ground. The creature's huge claws were now protruding from her lower jaw. Its fist enclosed her entire head, and as the light paused before it swung back, Mel watched as the giant wolf bit down on Ruby's head, cracking her skull as its teeth broke through it. The light moved, and she disappeared for the last time.

With Mel's senses rebooted, her flight instinct took over, and she ran through the gap in the tent. It didn't matter where, she just had to flee. As she headed into the darkness, she felt a warm sensation between her legs as her bladder emptied.

Howard watched as the werewolf bit through Ruby's scalp and cracked her skull, then discarded her body like a rag doll. It lifted its head back up, and turned its gaze on him. Blood spilled from its jaws. Ruby's blood. Howard wanted to run, to scream, but like in some childhood nightmare, he could do neither. All he could do was stare. In the swinging light Phil staggered back. His heel struck something and he lost his balance, flailing his arms around to stop his inevitable fall. He grabbed hold of a bedroom compartment wall and fell back, ripping the tent as he went down. The fabric now engulfed him. He was tangled up in it, and the more tried to free himself the more it wrapped around him. The tent tore along its seam. A large gap opened in its side and Howard used the distraction to escape. Wearing only light clothing and carrying absolutely nothing, he ran as fast as he could into the cold night.

With Howard gone and the tent now mostly collapsed, the werewolf grabbed Ruby's limp body. It dragged it out from the confines of the falling canvas, and disappeared. it was heading back towards Camera 4.

Phil eventually managed to set himself free of the scrambled tent frame. Pulling himself out, he picked up the last remaining light and shone it around him. The rear of the tent had completely collapsed. Only the front section, which held the equipment, remained intact. As he took a step forward his footing felt slippery, like he was standing in a think syrup. He held the light over his head and peered down. To his horror, his feet were in a large pool of blood. He followed the trail of blood until he came to its source. His stomach retched as he recognised Ruby's scalp; the ginger coils saturated with crimson blood. Tentatively he raised the light before him, and saw a trail of blood leading off into the night. It had taken her. With that realisation came another, just as chilling. He was alone. Howard and Mel had both run, and he didn't know what direction they had taken. He knew he had to leave too, but he couldn't navigate at night; not without technical help, and most of the equipment now lay smashed to pieces, including the walkie talkie. He should go *now,* before the werewolf came back for him. After hiding out tonight, he would walk back towards the inn at first light. He knew roughly what direction to go, and during the day he could pick up some landmarks here and there. His decision made, he set off from the camp.

Connar stood still; fear and confusion anchoring him to the spot. It had been a couple of minutes since he'd heard from Phil, though it felt much longer. He knew he couldn't just stand there - he would have to do *something.* He lowered the walkie talkie and set off towards camp, reassuring himself that the static and failure of the handsets was down to some storm somewhere or other. He quickened his pace, not wanting to think about the other possible reasons.

The light from the fire gave Connar a calming, settling feeling as he got closer to camp. All creatures were scared of fire. But as he crested the rise he began to make out the wreckage of the tent. By the time he got there panic had engulfed him. He pushed through the canvas tent flaps and froze, shaking with shock as he held the camera up and panned round the dark interior, trying to find any heat sources that would identify his crew. But he knew deep down that he was on his own. A feeling of dread flooded his entire body. He had been in the field enough times with tracking experts, to know that an apex predator always returned to an easy source of food, and right now he knew he was standing at ground zero. He quickly made his way out of the camp and headed back to where the car was parked, hoping he remembered the way correctly. If he got lucky he would make it by dawn. With this thought he too disappeared into the night.

7

Howard had run as far as he could. His legs burned with every stride and his feet were now dragging on the ground. His arms flapped limply by his side, his stomach ached, and sharp stabbing pains in his chest made breathing difficult. Each faltering step was more painful than the last. The adrenaline that had shot through his body as he'd fled, had carried him much farther than he would normally have managed, but now he had to stop. He desperately needed to rest. He sat down on the ground, and checked out his surroundings. His eyes were now accustomed to the light of the full moon, and he could see fairly well. He leaned back on the cold moorland heather, and rested, breathing deeply and slowly. With his head tilted back, he looked up to a sky full of stars. Only out in the wild could one see such a sky. A vast, deep sky full of natural wonder, like the awesome night skies back home in Oregon. You could never see a sky like this from the city. He watched as his breath left his body and dispersed against the back drop of the sky. It was simply beautiful, and for a while he felt at ease.

He knew he couldn't rest too long. He had to find a hiding place; somewhere he could cower in until morning. But what about the others?

He'd been worrying about them all the while he was running. They wouldn't be easy to find at night, with that... that thing prowling around. After witnessing the scene back at the tent, he still couldn't bring himself to say it was actually a werewolf. There had to be a scientific explanation - supernatural beings didn't exist. Surly the stories he'd read as a kid, and the TV shows, were just that - stories and shows. His mind struggled again with the concept of what had happened tonight. But right now he had to move, and find shelter. He'd think about it in the morning, and once he'd reached safety he'd bring the cops back to find his friends.

Mel ran into the old ruin that was once someone's home. The large stone house was still mostly intact; the brick structure and window frames fairly sound, but the windows and doors had long been broken. Running through the gap where the front door had once kept out the worst of the Welsh weather, she found herself at the bottom of a large staircase. The corridor in front of her carried on with two door frames to the right and another at the end, facing her. She edged slowly along the hallway. Despite the flow of fresh air from the open doorway, the smell in the house was rank. Through the first door frame she saw a large empty room with an enormous fireplace. The walls were filthy and the old carpet was badly stained. The foul smell from the room made her feel sick. She walked on to the next door frame and passed an almost identical room – this one somewhat cleaner and fresher. The last door frame led to the kitchen. Long abandoned, the large range oven was a rusting hulk, and the large oak table was covered in moss. Some of the kitchen cabinet doors had fallen from their mounts, and the rest were trying to break free. Mel didn't hang around. She headed back towards the front door, realising that this open house offered no safety. But she was exhausted. She urgently needed shelter, and she may not find a more suitable place. She stopped, and paused at the door space that led back outside and into the night. Then she decided to try upstairs.

She grabbed the banister. Placing one tentative foot on the first stair, she pushed forward and headed up to the landing; each wooden step groaning with its own distinctive creak or squeak. Up here the doors were still hung on their frames and some windows were still intact. The door in front of her was already open and she could see a pretty basic bathroom. Turning to her right she passed another open door - a bedroom, and as she entered she saw it was a child's bedroom. A boy's room. Model planes hung from the ceiling on long pieces of nylon, forever to fly round in circles until the house itself collapsed. A single bed stood alone in the far corner. Moss and dampness had long since claimed it for their own, along with the blue wallpaper which now hung in strips that were gradually peeling off and falling onto the mattress. Mel tried the next room. This one was smaller, and had been someone's office. A small table sat under the window, which by day would have offered remarkable views across the moorlands and into the woods.

She walked cautiously into the last bedroom. This was the double room. Mel could tell that in its day this room would have been a sanctuary to whoever had lived and worked here. Even through the cold light of the moon and the dampness that clung to its walls and windows, she could see it was once decadently decorated. She walked past the large king-sized bed to the double window that she imagined the masters of the house would once have gazed out of, after a quiet and peaceful night's sleep. As she turned away from the window she caught some movement out of the corner of her eye. Too frightened to look but too curious not to, she slowly turned her gaze back to the window, to look outside. Slowly she pushed her face to the glass, her nose touching the ice-cold surface. Turning her face to the right she looked down the outer wall and strained to see what distorted vision had peaked her curiosity. She searched for a while, but saw nothing. Convinced that she had imagined it, she shrugged her shoulders and walked away from the window.

Mel was beyond tired. She felt more exhausted than at any time she could recall. This wasn't the usual "bad day at the office" feeling; this was absolute total meltdown. She guessed this would be as good a place as any in which to settle for the night, and so she closed the bedroom door, turning the small brass handle that pushed across a small brass deadbolt. Feeling relatively secure, she sat on the floor and leaned against the wall, and tried to make herself comfortable. Her wet jeans stuck to her legs where she had urinated earlier, and now in the confines of the room, she noticed the smell. Pulling at the material to try and get it away from her skin, she attempted to get some relief from the discomfort. But the denim sprang back as soon as she let it go, and the horrible wet fabric stayed cold and tight against her skin. Sighing in defeat, she soon drifted into a light and restless sleep.

'Howard! Mel! Connar!' Phil shouted as loudly as he could.

Afraid and bewildered, his instincts were running on automatic. He had no rational thoughts or strategies for survival. He was alone, and that more than anything scared him enough to risk shouting for his friends. Like the others he had fled without collecting anything that would aid his survival through the night. Staggering along in the darkness he had no idea where he was or where he was going. He shouted again but this time he heard a reply.

'Phil?'

It was faint but he clearly heard his name. 'Over here,' he yelled. 'I'm over here!'

This time the response was louder. 'Stay where you are, I'm on my way to you.'

It was Howard, he recognised his voice. Phil sighed with relief. His shoulders sagged as the tension left them, and he smiled. He could see his friend now, making his way over to him. His silhouette was easily seen in the moonlight, gradually becoming larger as he came closer to him. Phil raised his arms above his head and started waving.

'Howard, I'm over here.'

'Where? I can't see you.'

Phil felt confused, and lowered his arms slightly. 'I'm right here, in front of you; straight ahead, keep walking straight ahead'

'I can't see you Phil there's nothing in front of me.'

'Howard I can see you there, keep walking straight?'

'Hang on... you gotta guide me to you, Phil You sound as if your behind me,' Howard shouted.

Now Phil was unsure, and all feelings of relief began to sink away from him. Howard's voice was coming from some distance behind him, while he continued to watch the figure in front of him grow in size. Then he saw the outline.

Panic, and feelings of dread and terror flooded his body, washing over his entire being. Now the outline in front of him was clear, and it was massive. It was running, not walking. Phil knew he should turn and flee, but his legs stayed fixed to the spot, as if in blocks of concrete. Now he could hear it; the soft thud on the ground as each step impacted. He could hear the snorting as it breathed rhythmically in time with its motion, and he could see the large head take shape against the backdrop of the full moon. Finally his legs freed themselves from his subconscious paralysis, and Phil turned to run. But he was too late. Suddenly it was on top of him. With one swing from its massive arm, its claws ripped through the flesh on his back.

The pain was excruciating, like a white hot knife slicing through him. He was flung through the air, and crashed down on his left side; his wrist taking the full weight of his body. It snapped instantly. Phil cried out in pain, rolling over onto his front. He pulled his right arm up to try and lift himself from the ground, but it was in vein. He felt the werewolf's weight on his torn back, and the claws struck again. This time they cut deep, the tips striking his spine. Phil screamed, flailing his right arm around in a desperate attempt to get the thing off him. Another swipe of the claws, this time across the back of his head. Now his scream was a high-pitched wail. A howl, like that of a wolf.

Howard followed Phil's shouts then his screams, and consequently arrived at the scene. Terrified, he dropped down into a ditch close by. He peered over the top and watched as the werewolf ripped Phil's back apart in a frenzied attack. This wasn't like a lion suffocating a Zebra, or like any other predator's hunt for food: This was a frantic, viscous, primal attack. The creature pinned Phil to the ground, its arms thrashing back and forth, ripping off chunks of flesh. Phil had no chance against this thing; this monster they had all set out to find, yet hadn't believed in. It was supposed to be another episode of the show, nothing more, and like all the other legends and mysteries, it wasn't supposed to be real. But it was real all right. As Howard watched it tear his friend apart, tears filled his eyes. He couldn't help him. It was a relief when Phil's screams of pain ceased.

He had no choice now but to stay low and keep an eye on where the werewolf would go next. He had to listen while the snapping and crunching of the feed continued. Desperate to vomit, he fought to keep it down. If he gave off any sounds or smells, then the same fate would become him. Phil's screams had masked his approach, but now there would be no cover. He had to remain perfectly still and absolutely quiet.

It seemed like an eternity before the creature had left Phil's body and headed away in the direction it had come from. Howard made sure that the figure's silhouette had long disappeared before he climbed from his make-shift trench and walked over to where his friend - or what was left him – lay. Howard brought his hand to his mouth but he could no longer resist the urge to vomit. He turned away and emptied his stomach.

Phil's back was gone. His skin was shredded and his spine had been snapped at the base of the skull and at the pelvis. Everything in between had been devoured. His head lay at an unnatural angle now that it had no support to keep straight. His internal organs had been ripped from his body cavity, and most of them had been consumed. The leftovers were strewn over the moors. Howard said, 'Sorry, buddy.' He felt he had let his friend down. He should have helped - tried to save him, at least done something, but he had witnessed this thing twice now, and he knew how powerful it was. It's actions were raw and ferocious; it was all of nature's worst creations in one, and deep down he knew if he'd done anything different, he too would be lying dismembered in this cold desolate place. He left the awful scene and headed away from the direction the werewolf had gone, to what he hoped was the direction of the car.

Connar stopped and checked his watch: 02:42. The illuminated figures glowed softly against the night, as he tried to get his bearings. He was pretty sure he was still heading towards the car. Tapping his pocket for what seemed like the thousandth time to make sure the keys were still in there, he set off again. He walked slowly and purposefully, making every footstep solid and well-placed. The last thing he needed now was to put his weight down on an uneven surface and sprain his ankle – or worse still, break it. As he continued on, clouds blew in from the west, and along with them a fine mist that seemed to hover then move sideways across the moors, shining silver against the light of the moon. He pulled his baseball cap out of his pocket and fixed it tightly on his head. Soon the soaked peek was dripping water in front of his face and onto his jacket. With his head tilted down and his hands pushed firmly into his pockets to guard against the driving spray, he pushed on. Step by step he assured himself that he was closer to the car, and safety.

Howard felt the fine spray of the mist before he saw it. 'Great, that's all I need - rain!' he muttered as he stumbled over the rough terrain. Deliberately staying off the rises or gradient peaks to make sure he would not be visible on any horizon, he trudged on. A little farther on he noticed a figure coming out of the gloom. It seemed like it was on course to intercept him. He stopped immediately, and re-assured himself that it hadn't spotted him. How could it have seen him? He was below the horizon line. But as the figure continued towards him he had a decision to make: to turn and flee - which would make a noise and leave a trail, and would no doubt end in a fall - or to do what he did last time: hide. Howard opted for the second choice. He scanned his immediate surroundings, trying - in the ever decreasing light smothered by the low clouds - to find a trench or fox hole or somewhere to drop down out of sight. Eventually he found a ditch, and dived in. Curled up in the small space, he tried to breathe quietly, but that proved difficult. His adrenaline had kicked in again. His muscles ached and twitched and his heart felt like it would burst from his chest any moment now. He willed his body to calm down, but terror kept his heart pounding. He knew the werewolf's senses were likely to be highly tuned – he'd confidently told everyone that, back at camp. The *werewolf?* He still had trouble acknowledging that it was a werewolf. Suddenly he was aware of footsteps close by, as they squelched in the soft moorland heather. Closer and closer they came, until he thought they would land on top of him. Pulling himself tighter into a foetal position, he could do nothing now but close his eyes and wait for the inevitable. The footsteps approached, and he held his breath.

After an eternity, the stamping footsteps passed and moved on. Howard listened with relief as the sound faded into the distance. He breathed out a sigh of relief, and peered above the ditch. But what he saw wasn't the back of the monster - it was Connar! Howard scrambled to his feet and climbed out of the ditch.

'Connar!' he called through clenched jaws, attempting the impossible feat of shouting and whispering at the same time.

Connar stopped and turned around. 'Howard, is that you?'

Howard rushed over to Connar and grabbed his arms. 'Jesus, am I glad to see you!'

'Likewise,' Connar said, visibly relieved. 'Do you know what happened back at the camp? Where the rest of the guys? I haven't seen anyone.'

Howard let go of Connar, placed his hands on his own hips, and bowed his head. 'I don't know where Mel is. She took off when that thing attacked. It got Ruby - in the tent.'

'What about Phil?' Connar asked.

'It got him too. I saw it happen.' Howard started to cry. He pulled his arm up and wiped the tears from his face before continuing. 'It just ripped him to pieces, he didn't stand a chance. It pulled his fucking spine out. I mean, what kind of animal does that?' Anger surfaced through his grief, and his emotions left him feeling drained. 'I should have helped him. I should have tried, but I just hid. I should have done something.'

Connar's tears fell silently. He put a hand on Howard's shoulder. 'You couldn't have done anything Howard, it would have ripped you apart too. This isn't some bar fight you could have broken up. This thing - it's supernatural. It's something that shouldn't be here, it shouldn't exist.'

Howard pulled away, shrugging his shoulder from Connar's hold. 'Yeah right, it shouldn't exist,' Howard yelled, 'but you had to stay, you had to find proof!'

Connar tried to calm him down. 'Shhh, quiet! You'll bring it to us.'

In the dim light Connar saw Howard's mood change from fury back to sorrow.

'I'm sorry Connar, I shouldn't have said that. We all decided to stay – all except Ruby. This wasn't just your call.'

A peaceful silence descended over them for a few moments.

'Come on,' Connar said, 'we gotta keep moving - see if we can get to the car. Let's go.'

Howard nodded his agreement, and walked

quietly by Connar's side as they headed in the direction of where they believed the car was parked.

Mel felt a tickling sensation on her cheek. In her dazed and sleepy state she wiped it with the back of her hand, but as soon as she cleared it, it returned, this time rousing her to consciousness. She rubbed at her cheek again as her eyes strained to focus in the dark surroundings. Gradually the old derelict bedroom came into view and she remembered where she was, and more importantly, why she was there. The memories shot through her like a bolt of electricity, and she sat upright. Now aware of the dripping water that had wakened her, she looked up to the large hole in the roof. The moon was now directly overhead but it was only visible in small segments, as clouds now covered most of it. She yawned, stretched, and stood up to think things through. She felt trapped - there was nowhere else to go. But with the door closed and locked she felt reasonably secure here. She looked out of the window, and saw the clouds drifting over the house. She checked her watch, pressing the button that illuminated the dial: its soft green glow showed 04:52. A sigh escaped as she wandered back to the spot where she'd slept sitting on the floor, wishing that time would move faster.

She sat back down to wait for dawn.

The werewolf was still hunting; its thirst for blood and natural urge to kill driving it on to find more food. It moved in circular hunting patterns, changing from two legs to four as it sniffed, looked and listened for prey. Standing on its hind legs its right eye caught something and its head shot round in an instant. It saw a faint light in the distance - a soft glow that seemed to float off the ground. It cocked its head to one side; its mind trying to make sense of this dim green glow. Then it was gone. The werewolf stood motionless, staring into the black of the night, taking in large gulps or air as it sniffed for any clues. There was a smell coming from the direction of the light – a familiar smell of prey. It immediately dropped onto all four legs, and set off on its quest for food.

The smell became stronger as the beast bounded over the landscape with ease, its long powerful legs making light work of the heavy sodden moors. The werewolf was now in full hunting mode, and all of its senses were focused on one thing: the scent. That scent led it straight to the abandoned house, where it had feasted many times in the past. As it approached the house it slowed to stop, lifting itself back onto its rear legs. It raised its head and sniffed the air, pinpointing the exact source of the scent. The huge beast threw its head back and howled - a long piercing howl; a primeval noise that announced it presence and its intentions to all.

Mel woke with a start. She bolted upright, her wits kicking in fast. The second howl was louder, more threatening, and it seemed to come from just outside the house. Her worst fear was upon her. The evil creature that had killed Ruby was closing in, and all she could do was play a waiting game. Soon the werewolf would find her, and death would follow.

8

Connar and Howard stopped dead in their tracks.

'Oh shit, what was that?' Howard said, as they heard the first howl.

'Quiet!' Connar snapped, putting his finger to his lips.

The second howl was more haunting. Howard grabbed Connar's arm to pull him along but Connar pulled free from his grip.

'Wait!' he told Howard.

'Wait for what? Jesus, man, let's go!'

Connar held him back, frustration bursting through his being. 'Just wait a second. We gotta think first before we do anything stupid. Okay, the howl seemed to come from that direction, over there.' He pointed ahead, to the left.

'Yeah, so?'

'So if we know what direction it's in, we know we're okay to continue heading towards the car – we don't have to turn and run back. And we also know the werewolf's a fair distance away.'

Howard's posture slumped, and he sighed. 'Okay, that kinda makes sense. What's over there anyway, do you know?'

Connar shook his head. 'I dunno, and I ain't gonna find out. Let's go.'

He headed off in the direction they had being travelling, looking back to make sure that

Howard was following.

Alone and terrified, Mel had an overwhelming feeling of dread and doom - as if death itself was standing in the room with her, waiting to collect her soul. Putting both hands flat against the door she checked the lock once again, knowing that the small brass bolt would not keep the powerful creature out. She looked around the room desperately trying to find something she could jam against the door, but the only object in the room was the old bed. If she dragged it over the noise would give away her location. And besides, if *she* could move the bed, then the werewolf could move it too. She listened with her ear to the door... she could hear it moving around downstairs, its large claws tapping on the flag stones as it walked. Maybe it wouldn't come upstairs. It might just look around downstairs, and leave. Mel's mind was working overtime, trying to figure out how she could possibly make it to daylight. She heard the tapping move and then stop... now there was nothing, no sound at all, only the whisper of the wind as it blew through the old damaged roof. She heard a creak. Then another. Then a succession of squeaks and creaks, telling her that the thing was coming up the stairs. She peered through the cracks in the old door frame, as each footstep impacted on the next stair. Creak, thump, scrape - she could hear the stairs groaning in protest under the weight of the giant beast.

The back of its head came into view first. Then its shoulders. It stopped, raising its head as it sniffed her out. Its spun round to face her, and its eyes looked straight at her. She jumped back, letting out a cry. Holding her hands to her mouth, she backed away from the door. She heard the werewolf climb the rest of the stairs, and then make its way towards the room. As Mel placed one foot silently behind the other, still backing away, her eyes filled with tears. An overwhelming feeling of sadness flooded through her as she realised her was situation was hopeless. She could hear its deep breathing now, right outside the door.

The first bang on the door sounded as if the werewolf was testing its strength. Mel was now standing with her back pressed hard against the back wall. Suddenly she had an idea – if she could drop down from the window and run, that might give her enough time to escape. Without hesitation she ran to the window. She struggled to push the window up in its loose, rotting frame. 'Oh... oh no! Open!' she screamed in panic as she tried to raise the window, but it seemed to be jammed shut. 'Fuck!' she yelled, frantically rattling the frame. With one last, almighty effort, causing her to cry out in a rasping shriek, she pulled at the window. Suddenly it shot up, shuddering the whole rickety frame. Mel climbed onto the sill, planning to lower herself down to a height she could drop from, but as she readied herself the second impact hit the door, and this time it flew open.

She saw it only for the briefest of moments before her balance took her over the edge. As she fell Mel remembered aspects of her life long since forgotten, and a sense of well-being washed away all her fear. A soft smile appeared on her face just before she hit the ground. Then with a dull thud, everything went black.

Mel felt nothing of the carnage inflicted by the beast, upon her lifeless body.

As Connar and Howard pushed on, low cloud made it impossible to make a clear and accurate judgement about which direction they should take. Now and then the moon would shine like a small torch, giving them just enough light to see where they were going, but then as if to tease them it would disappear and leave them lost. They hadn't spoken much since they'd hiked out of the moors, towards the car. They really didn't have much to say; partly because they were too tired, but mostly because they were afraid that the sound of their voices would give away their position. Connar checked his watch again: it flashed 05:24.

'What time is it?' Howard asked.

'Almost 5.30.'

'Not too long till daybreak,' Howard said. It was hope, not knowledge.

As they continued their trudge across the now sodden ground, the initial dull thud of their footsteps had long been replaced with the squelching sound of soaked moss and heather on top of wet mud. The heavy going made their legs ache. Thick clots of earth stuck to their boots, weighing them down, and their jackets were soaked through. The fine mist of rain seemed to penetrate every inch of their person, making them feel heavy, awkward, and miserable. The adrenaline that had previously coursed through them was now depleted, and like a child coming down from a sugar rush, they felt exhausted. But both men knew they had to continue on their way. The sun would rise in a couple of hours, and they should reach the car about then, Connar reckoned. He had managed to evade the werewolf so far, and he'd risk a bet on his luck holding out. Hopefully he and Howard would be able to tell their story and warn others that some extremely terrifying creatures were not just stories or the images of nightmares, but they are real and that they roamed the earth.

The clouds finally started to clear and once again the stars filled the sky in a beautiful, sparkling array, as if watching over them. But after a few wondrous moments, they seemed to fade and lose their vitality.

'Look over there,' Connar said, pointing to his left.

Howard saw the moon starting to dip behind the horizon.

'You see that?' Connar said. 'It won't be long before the sun rises.'

They gave each other a reassuring smile, and continued walking at a faster pace.

Eventually they reached flat grassland. Stepping out from the last patches of heather, they both knew the car wasn't far away. As Connar stepped his foot slipped on the wet grass and a hot pain ran across his right ankle as he went down.

'Jesus Christ!' Connar yelled in pain

'Are you alright?'

'Help me up I'll be fine, but you'll have drive' Connar said as he handed Howard the keys

As they rounded the corner they could see it ahead of them - the silver Ford Galaxy that would now become their fortress. Connar reached down into his pocket, feeling around for the keys. The feel of the plastic tag the rental company had fastened to the key, was very reassuring. He pulled out the key and pressed the little button, and instantly the car greeted them with its flashing indicators, unfolding mirrors and the sound of the doors unlocking. It reminded Howard of an excited puppy waiting for its master's return.

They climbed into the car, slamming the doors

shut behind them.

'Thank god for that!' Howard said.

'God had nothing to do with it,' Connar said, as he slipped the credit card shaped key into the slot and pressed the red start button. The comforting sound of the diesel engine ticking over, filled them with relief - the sound of the 21st. century.

'Can we please just go now?' Howard urged Connar.

'Sure. I was just taking a moment, you know?'

'I know. We're leaving a lot behind.'

Howard slipped the car into gear and released the handbrake. As he reversed the Galaxy round on full lock, the tyres squelched and began to sink in the wet mud.

'Don't get stuck! Smooth and easy Howard' Connar warned.

Howard went easy on the gas and released the clutch slowly, to prevent the front wheels from spinning. The nose of the car started to pull round. Slowly he allowed the steering wheel to centre, until they were facing the lane that had brought them here. He switched on the headlamps and high beams, lighting up the path in front of them. Then he checked his rear view mirror and pulled away. The eerie red glow of the tail lights left a cold chill inside him.

The impact came suddenly, before Connar had finished yelling 'Watch out!' The beast had sprung from the glowing red void left behind by the car's tail lights. It smashed into the passenger's side, breaking the windows and badly denting the side doors. Howard's hands were shaken off the steering wheel, his head hit the side window, and his feet left the pedals with the force of the impact.

'Jesus Howard, go go *go!*' Connar was hysterical.

Howard now had a dilemma. He knew he had to get out - and quick, but he also knew that if he went too fast the car would skid or bog down in the mud. The low profile tyres were good for tarmac but no good for off-road. He had to think fast. He decided to put his foot to the floor and make a run for it. As the engine roared and the car took off, the beast struck again, shuddering the vehicle so hard that it rocked violently. Howard fought to keep control of the unstable, speeding car. Suddenly Connar screamed in pain, as the beast's sharp teeth sank deep into his shoulder. His cry shattered the air, and Howard turned to see the huge head of the werewolf inside the car as it ran alongside it. The creature released its grip and snarled, ready to take another bite, but Howard turned the wheel to the left and sandwiched the thing between the car and the high thick stone wall that ran parallel to the lane.

They heard the animal snarl and howl as the hard rocks dug into its flesh. It pushed forward against the car, and Howard felt it slip on the soft mud. He forced the steering wheel round further, and this time the werewolf lost its footing and fell under the car. The back end of the Galaxy rose up as the rear wheel ran over the werewolf's leg, then the car jolted back onto its four wheels. Howard sped ahead, looking in his rear mirror to see if the creature was still alive. Just visible in the red glow of the tail lights, the beast lifted its head and howled its agony. Howard looked away, but then glanced back, too anxious to not know what was happening. But the beast was out of sight.

Howard noticed the first glimmers of light breaking through. Now he could reassure his friend.

'Hold on Connar, I'll get help soon. Just hold on.'

Connar's reply was weak. He was holding his injured shoulder as tightly as he could, but blood still flowed freely from it.

'Okay,' he whispered. 'Hurry, Howard. Please hurry.'

They followed the green lane to its end, then turned onto the road that would lead them back to the inn. As the sun rose in the early morning sky Howard pulled into the inn's car park. With the damaged passenger door jammed shut, he dragged Connar as gently as possible, across the seats and out the driver's side. Only then did he realise the extent of his injuries. A deep laceration ran across his left shoulder, with clear puncture marks where the werewolf's teeth had embedded deep into his muscle. Connar flung his good arm around Howard's neck, and Howard supported his weight as they staggered towards the inn. Connar collapsed as soon as they were inside.

'Help! I need help here. Can somebody help me please?' Howard shouted, as he struggled to hold the unconscious Connar. But the bar was empty. Empty and dark, just as he remembered it to be on their arrival. That seemed like a lifetime ago, yet it was only a couple of days ago.

Evan burst in through the swing doors, lifted the hatch in the bar, and hurried over to the two men. Connar was lying on his back on the floor, and his breathing was laboured. Howard was kneeling beside him, looking up at Evan as he approached. He looked traumatised, and spoke in a breathless, trembling voice.

'Can you help us, Evan? He... he needs help.'

Evan looked down at them, nodding his head slowly. 'Bring him through here, lad.'

He helped Howard to lift Connar and carry him through to the kitchen, behind the bar. They laid him on the large solid wood table in the middle of the room. Evan studied Connar's injury, tutting and shaking his head.

'You found it then. By the looks of things, I imagine it found you. I told you no good would come of it.'

Howard slumped onto a chair, and leaned forward on the table for support. 'Yes, we found it, and we've documented it. All I have to do is go back there with the police and get my equipment. I'm sure the officers will wanna ask you some questions about what you know.'

Evan smiled. 'Equipment, you say? What equipment?'

Howard looked confused. 'Our cameras and computers - you know, the equipment we used to track the creature and record the evidence of its existence.'

Evan fetched the first-aid box from one of the kitchen cabinets, and tended to Connar's wounds. First he cleaned the wounds with antiseptic liquid, then - to Howard's horror - he took out a needle and thread and started suturing a gash. Howard sat open-mouthed as he watched, but he said nothing. Evan seemed to know what he was doing. In fact he looked suitably experienced as he skilfully closed the gaps in Connar's flesh.

'Well it's like this,' Evan said, still focussed on his task, 'what with you going up there, I got the mountain rescue and police to search the area. The storm, you see – they were looking for you because of the storm. We wanted to make sure you were okay, but there was no sign of anyone, and they never found any equipment. Nothing, I say. No sign of anything. I thought maybe you'd changed your mind – heeded my warning, and left.'

'We were up there, for sure. My friends were killed – Phil, Ruby, I... I don't know what happened to Mel... '

'The pretty dark haired girl'

'Yes, Mel is she here? Is she okay? What happened to her? '

'The beast happened to her lad, I told you, I warned you but your like all the rest with your fancy equipment, thinking it will save you... '

Evan gripped the thread between his teeth and pulled, breaking it. Connar groaned, but he didn't wake up.

'There, he'll be as good as new and sooner than you may think lad' Evan said proudly, admiring his work.

Howard stood up. 'What do you mean, nothing was found?' he said, his voice strained in exasperation. 'They must have found our camp site – our tents, our equipment, our stuff. And we made an enormous camp fire – they must have seen the remains of the fire.'

Evan stood straight and looked him in the eye. 'Listen here, boy. There's nothing up there. You found nothing and left nothing.'

Howard walked up to him. 'Is that a threat, old man? You trying to stop me telling my story? What the fuck are you gonna do? I can bring a shit storm on this fucking place, you know. I'll bring every American news station down on you. I'll spread rumours on the web, you'll be fucking over-run with people like me!'

Evan stood his ground. 'Oh I don't think so, lad. Mainstream media won't touch a story like this. They'll laugh it off – make a fool of you. Outsiders don't believe it, you see. You didn't believe it yourself, did you? You see, maybe they did find bodies and maybe they didn't, but I'll tell you this...' Evan's face flushed with anger, his frown sinister and menacing, his lips curled in a snarl. 'You start shouting your big Yankee mouth off and it'll come to light that you murdered those poor souls. It'll be you that gets the shit storm over you.'

Before Howard could think of a reply the kitchen door opened and two men walked in, one in police uniform and the other a larger man, dressed in casual clothing. The latter had a deep cut on the left side of his face, and bandages all the way down his left arm and leg. His gaze was threatening. Howard had a feeling of deja vu – this guy seemed somehow familiar.

Evan spoke to the police officer, with a sarcastic undertone in his voice. 'I was just telling this fine young man, that if he started blabbing on about some make- believe monster running around these hills, the truth would have to come out. It would be a shame to have to tell the truth about what he did to those poor young women and that unfortunate lad.'

The officer smiled at Howard as he spoke. 'It certainly would, Evan. Of course, if he keeps his mouth shut it would be nothing more than a tale of three tourists who walked out there unprepared, and were never found. It's amazing how many times that happens in these parts.'

Howard had nowhere to turn. The local police were in on it. If this cop filed an official report that he was the one who killed Phil, Mel and Ruby, he couldn't defend himself with the true account of their deaths. No-one would believe the truth. He knew he was beaten. He'd have to live with the secret. Connar's survival was some degree of consolation, but knowing what really happened and never being able to tell anyone, would be hell. He bowed his head and sighed in defeat.

Connar began to regain consciousness. Still semi-alert, he was helped off the table by two protectors of the Welsh werewolf legend.

Howard immediately helped Connar out to the car, and made straight for Heathrow. Thankfully they had left their passports in the glove compartment of the car. By the time they'd reached the airport Connar injuries had mysteriously already started to recover enough to travel home.

Epilogue

Fourteen months had passed since their return from Wales, and their lives had regained some degree of normality. The official report stated that Philip Hughes, Melanie Ward and Ruby Lauren had died of exposure somewhere out on the Welsh moorlands, and that only a few of their personal belongings had been found. The chance of finding their bodies was reported as "slim."

After a long battle with the network, who wanted to continue *Myth Seekers*, Connar sold the rights of the show to them and walked away. He had got enough money to retire to Carson, a small town on the banks of the Hood River.

His injuries had healed remarkably well, with only a few small scars to remind him of his ordeal. Like Howard, he wanted to forget what had happened that night, but it wasn't easy. In the beginning their restless nights were plagued by recurring nightmares which left them exhausted. But as the weeks passed, Connar stopped having such disturbing episodes, and returned to full health. Now his family and friends thought him to be in better health than he'd ever been.

Howard had moved to LA. The larger the city, the less chance there would be of something lurking in the shadows, he reckoned. Paranoia was foremost in his mind these days.

He settled back in the large reclining chair he'd bought when he had moved into his new apartment. He now lived in a gated community, with security guards and key numbered entrances to all the housing units, reinforced steel doors and CCTV. He pushed the power button on the TV remote, and the large HD screen came to life. An advertisement came on as he took the first swig of his cold beer. Then the show started.

"This week on Myth Seekers, with an all new team of investigators, we explore strange events around Carson, Washington State, where the locals have reported mutilated pets, strange sightings, peculiar foot prints and bizarre howls in the night."

***

Dennis, how was the ending?

Other Titles Available:

Yesterday's Flight

When a Dinosaur fossil is unearthed in the Badlands of America, the last thing Susan Lavey expects to find beside it is the tail section of an airliner – apparently the cause of the dinosaur's death. Together with Bruce Ackland - a chief air crash investigator - they must find out how this could have happened, and what became of the passengers on board.

William Relford was flying to yet another meeting, but this time it was to hand in his notice. He had worked in sales for as long as he liked to remember, and now it was time for a change. But destiny has a way of changing things, and now it was about to bring three people together in a race for the truth, and for one, even survival.

The Harvesting

It is estimated that 250,000 people vanish in the UK each year.

It is estimated that 820,000 people vanish in the USA each year.

It is not known how many people vanish world-wide each year.

But on November 25th at 17:37 GMT, 88.7% of

the earth's population will vanish in one night,
and for one man the search will begin.
  Will you be one of them?

www.martynellington.com
August 1st 2012

Ruby's Research was taken from Britain's Worst Real Monsters:

Written by Nicholas Pells and published by Wingman37 Publications.

Gladys Green 1912 – 2012

Lightning Source UK Ltd.
Milton Keynes UK
UKOW042338120912

198930UK00001B/8/P